GOOD ROCKIN' TONIGHT

BANTAM NEW FICTION

GOOD ROCKIN' TONIGHT

A COLLECTION
OF SHORT STORIES
WILLIAM HAUPTMAN

BANTAM BOOKS
TORONTO · NEW YORK · LONDON · SYDNEY · AUCKLAND

GOOD ROCKIN' TONIGHT
A Bantam Book / October 1988

Library of Congress Cataloging-in-Publication Data

Hauptman, William, 1945–
  Good rockin' tonight.

  (Bantam new fiction)
  I. Title.
PS3558.A758G66   1988   813'.54   88-47510
ISBN 0-553-34557-5

Published simultaneously in the United States and Canada

Bantam Books are published by Bantam Books, a division of Bantam Doubleday Dell Publishing Group, Inc. Its trademark, consisting of the words "Bantam Books" and the portrayal of a rooster, is Registered in U.S. Patent and Trademark Office and in other countries. Marca Registrada. Bantam Books, 666 Fifth Avenue, New York, New York 10103.

PRINTED IN THE UNITED STATES OF AMERICA

This book is dedicated to Marjorie and Cooter
and I'd also like to express my gratitude to Gloria Loomis and
Deborah Futter

"He was too strong for me. He had women on his side."
—Ibsen, *Peer Gynt*

CONTENTS

GOOD ROCKIN'
TONIGHT

The year Elvis died was a strange year, and I remember it not only because of what happened to my brother, Bubba, but because that was the year we had our first transsexual here in Nortex. Bobby Joe Pitts, who worked for Builders' Supply, told the wife and kids he still loved them, but he couldn't stand it any longer: He'd always felt like a woman in a man's body and wanted to go to Houston for a sex-change operation.

He'd been saving money for years in a secret account and was all ready to go through with it. But the doctor in Houston was cautious. He told Bobby Joe he should try wearing women's clothes for six months before the operation, since there would be no going back. So Bobby Joe came to our church, First Methodist, looking something like Mary Tyler Moore. His family took it hard. The preacher suggested, after the services, that he go to the Unitarian church instead, where they took homosexuals and drug addicts. Bobby Joe stormed out, saying we were hypocrites and had no spirit of Christian love.

The first nice day rolled around, he was out at Skyline Country Club, just like every other year, for his eighteen holes of Saturday morning golf. Harley Otis told me when I walked into the locker room. Said Bobby Joe expected to play in the club tournament, but against the women. Harley was disgusted. "I guess it had to happen here," he said, snorting and throwing his shoes all the way across the room, where they hit the big picture of Arnold Palmer on the locker room wall.

I felt sorry for Bobby Joe and went out to where he was teeing off alone. He said he was no different from that doctor who became a lady tennis pro. "They're just threatened," he said primly. About that time, Harley drove past in his electric cart and shouted out, asking Bobby Joe if he was for the ERA. Bobby Joe shot him the finger.

That night I sat on my patio, drinking Jack Daniel's and looking up at the stars. Through the sliding glass doors, I could see my wife watching her favorite program. Hell, I could see Bobby Joe's point of view. I might like being a woman myself if I looked like Mary Tyler Moore. Trouble was, I wouldn't; and neither would Bobby Joe. I doubted any amount of plastic surgery could do the trick. My wife, alone there in the den, laughed at something on television, and I felt like a ghost. I decided the world was changing so fast nobody could keep up with it.

I'm a doctor myself, obstetrics and gynecology, and I've got a little office across the street from the hospital. Who should come see me the next day but my old high school sweetheart, Nadine MacAfee, whom I'd seen no more than two or three times in all the years since graduation. But my heart still stopped when I saw her there in the reception room.

In my office, she told me she'd like to get off the pill and try some other form of contraception. She dropped hints about her loneliness and talked nostalgically about the days when we'd gone steady; and I soon realized she was looking for romance. I was so nervous I thought I was going to stammer for the first time in years, and resorted to a trick the speech therapist had taught me: flipping my pencil up and catching it, not thinking too much about what I was saying.

"Look, Nadine," I said finally, "if it's all the same, I'd rather not examine you. But I can recommend another doctor."

"That's all right, Ross," she said. "I understand."

She had once been so shy, and this was a pretty bold thing for her to do. But I had never gone all the way with Nadine in high school and I wasn't about to now. I wanted to keep her the way she was in my memory—full of innocence and mystery. So I took out the bottle I keep in my desk drawer, we had a drink, and I got her talking about her kids, my pencil flipping just like old Johnny Carson's.

When I showed her out, my brother, Bubba, who was a big wheel with the Prudential Insurance Company, was sitting in the reception room with a long face on. When I asked him what was wrong, he told me Elvis had died and we had to celebrate his passing away. "The King is gone," he said, "and nobody will ever replace him." I sent the rest of my patients home.

I hadn't known Elvis was so important to my brother, but then I really didn't know Bubba anymore. We played golf now and then, but our wives hated each other, which seems to be the rule, not the exception; so we never saw each other socially, not at all.

We drove out to a bar in the new shopping mall, where neither of us had ever been. Thank God It's Friday's it was called, and I think it was supposed to look like Greenwich Village.

"What the hell has happened here?" my brother said.

"How do you mean, Bubba?"

"What's happened to this town? Why is everyone pretending they're in New York City?"

"I don't know, Bubba; I guess it's television."

To me, the whole shopping mall was a depressing place. Nobody had been able to rest until we got one, just like every other town. There must have been a thousand editorials in the paper about it. On the way in, we'd passed droves of sad-looking teenagers hanging out around the fountain, and I'd thought how much happier we looked out at the Pioneer Drive-In, in our cars. But everyone was proud of the mall as they could be, and who was wrong, them or me?

Harley Otis was there, right in the thick of it, wearing polyester pants, white loafers with gold chains, a leather jacket, and a Dacron shirt with the collar spread out on his shoulders. There was also a little gold chain around his neck.

"Who you tryin' to look like, Harley?" my brother asked. "The Six Million Dollar Man?"

Harley took it as a compliment and started telling us how he'd just gotten back from a Successful Life course in Dallas where he'd learned the importance of a Positive Mental Attitude. "You've got to set goals for yourself," he said.

"What's your goal, Harley?"

"Right now, I'm buckin' for president of Kiwanis. But my immediate goal is to get into Tina Eubank's pants."

I looked over and there was Tina, twice divorced, standing by the jukebox. It didn't look like he'd have too much trouble. "Y'all have a nice day," Harley said, and slid toward her.

Then we drove out the Fort Worth Highway, my brother talking about everything he hated, from women's lib to *People* magazine. I hadn't seen him like this for years. There had been a time, when I was in med school and my brother was driving a truck, when he developed all sorts of theories about why this country was going to pieces. He also claimed to have seen UFOs and talked to them on his CB. I finally diagnosed the problem when I discovered he was taking "L.A. turnarounds"—those biphetamine capsules truckers use on long hauls. Once he started working for the Prudential, he settled down and that side of him disappeared.

But now he was driving too fast and talking crazy, like he used to; looking around at everything and not liking what he saw. Just then, I heard a siren and saw flashing blue lights, and a highway patrol car pulled us over.

It was Floyd Simms, whom I hadn't seen in maybe fifteen years. "Could I see your operator's license?" he asked, all business, holding his metal clipboard.

"It's Bubba Moody, Floyd."

"You were exceeding a posted speed limit of fifty-five miles per hour, and it looks to me like you got alcoholic beverages in the car."

"Floyd, don't you remember? We took shop together."

"Yeah, I remember. But shitfire, Bubba, you were driving like a bat."

"Floyd, Elvis died today."

"I heard."

"My brother and I are drinking to his memory. Don't give me the cold shoulder, Floyd. Have a drink with us and let's remember all the good and bad old days."

"Well, I do get off duty in half an hour," Floyd said, looking across the car at me and grinning. "That really you, Ross?"

5

*   *   *

Then the three of us went out to the old colored man's place. It was my brother's idea. You could have knocked me over with a stick when I saw it was still there, the little redbrick building with the sign that said HOT PIT COOKED BAR-B-QUE.

The old man himself, who had a big stomach and a pencil mustache (Fats Domino, we had called him), opened the counterweighted lid of the stove. Inside was at least a chine of beef. He cut off slabs and put them on bread. Then he added half a green onion and a wedge of long-horn cheese and wrapped it all in butcher paper.

We carried our sandwiches to a table, and the other customers, all colored (black, I corrected myself), sort of looked at us without looking at us, for Floyd still wore his highway patrol uniform; then got up and left, dropping their trash in the garbage can on the way out.

"See, big brother?" Bubba said. "The past is still here, all around us."

I couldn't take my eyes off my sandwich. It sat there on the tabletop, which was bare except for a Louisiana Hot Sauce bottle full of toothpicks. Grease spotted the butcher paper. I took a bite and it ran down my chin. Lord, it was good.

Bubba returned from the cooler with three bottles of Royal Crown Cola, the old-style bottles with the yellow pyramids on them. "Look at that," he said softly, staring at his bottle. "Would you look at that?" Then he drank it.

"What are you up for, Floyd?" he said.

"My wife's going to be wondering where I am," Floyd said, and when Bubba gave him a sour look, added, "Shitfire, Bubba, there's a good program on tonight. About Vince Lombardi."

I nodded. "My wife's not home. Tonight's her yoga

class. Y'all could come over and watch it." What was I saying "y'all" for? I hadn't said "y'all" in years.

"What's so important about Vince Lombardi?" Bubba said. "You never knew him. A night like this comes once in a lifetime, and tonight the three of us are going to the Cotton Bowling Palace."

So we drove on down to the long, low building on Holiday Creek, full of the odor of paste wax and the thunder of balls; and the same people were there who had always been there, roughnecks and refinery workers and railroad brakemen. I was clumsy at first, dropping the ball on the lane with a thud; but Bubba was greasing them in right off. We didn't bother to keep score. None of us could remember how. We just bowled, and I relaxed, for by now the evening was lost, anyway, watching Bubba cut up, bowling like Don Carter, and so forth. He could always impersonate anyone he wanted. Mom said his version of me was deadly. When he came over and dropped down beside me in one of the green plastic chairs, I felt a stab of brotherhood and socked him on the arm, the way I would have in the old days.

"Hey, Bubba," I said. "You old son of a bitch."

"You're not sorry you're not home watching the life of old Vince Lombardi?"

"No, Bubba. I genuinely enjoyed this night."

"Life is a road."

"Yes, Bubba. Life is a road." I waited for him to finish, so drunk the bowling balls sounded like they were rolling through my head.

"Once I thought I knew who I was and where I was going. I could see the road ahead. But I lost my way."

Floyd was out on the lane, yelling. A pin had fallen outside the gate, and when nobody appeared to help, he

7

walked up the lane, slipping and falling down, and got it himself. People were laughing at him.

"There was only one person of our time who never stopped. Who became the person he dreamed of becoming."

"Who's that?"

"Elvis," my brother said.

Do you know what he did then? He stepped up to the booth where you got your shoes and where they called your number when your lane was ready. He grabbed the microphone away from the fat lady who was sitting there and sang "Love Me Tender" to her. It started as a joke, but this was the day Elvis had died, and when he finished, the place was dead quiet. Then everyone applauded and started shouting, "More, more," and I was shouting, too. And he did sound exactly like Elvis, although I never thought he looked like him at all. I thought he looked more like Conway Twitty.

One year later to the day, I was riding down Highway 82 in a white Cadillac Eldorado. The oil-well pumping jacks nodded in the fields, the blacktop shimmered in the heat, and in the front seat was my brother Bubba, wearing a white jump suit with silver studs, his hair dyed black. The sign on the side of the car read:

EL TEX AS

BUBBA MOODY KING OF ROCK AND ROLL

NORTEX' OWN ELVIS

Floyd Simms was driving, wearing Las Vegas shades and the Robert Hall suit Bubba had bought him at the Hub Clothing Store.

Bubba had done better than I would have believed, perfecting his act at Kiwanis and Rotary dances. He'd also done benefits for the crippled and retarded children, which people liked, and borrowed enough money to lease this Eldorado just like the one Elvis had. Now we were on our way to the first stop on Bubba's summer tour, which was to end at Six Flags Over Texas. There was to be a convention of Elvis Presley impersonators, and Bubba intended to prove he was the best in the world.

"This is the life, isn't it?" he said, looking back at me and grinning. "Man, sometimes I feel so good I've got to go out and take a walk through K-Mart to bring myself down."

We stopped at the Cow Lot in Nocona, where Bubba bought a pair of ostrich-hide boots and gave the owner an eight-by-ten autographed glossy photo, which he thumbtacked on the wall next to the photos of Willie Nelson, Arthur Godfrey, Howard Hughes, and all the other celebrities who, down through the years, had bought Nocona boots.

When we got back in the car, Bubba said, "Floyd, I think I'm going to ask you to dye your hair red so I can call you Red West." That was Elvis's bodyguard. Bubba really wanted to make the act authentic.

We came to a billboard that said we were eight miles from Decatur, home of Dico Sausage, and showed a pair of rolling dice. "Pull over, Floyd," Bubba said.

He struck a karate pose in front of the billboard and Floyd took his picture with the Polaroid Swinger. I was getting back in the car when I heard a buzz just like an electric alarm clock going off.

"Christ, Bubba, what the hell you doing?" Floyd said. Bubba had picked up a baby rattlesnake out of the ditch and was making like he was going to kiss it, holding it inches away from his lips.

"Get a picture, get a picture," he shouted, laughing like an idiot.

We drove on through more North Texas and finally into Decatur, where a banner across the street proclaimed Bubba's show. "The King is here," my brother said.

Floyd parked and we walked into the high school, across the street from the red-granite courthouse. The band was already setting up. Down in the dressing room, Bubba put on his makeup and I sat on a box of textbooks in the corner and watched. Already you could hear people filling the auditorium upstairs. "Sounds like a good crowd," Bubba said, gluing on his fake sideburns.

Then a local disc jockey appeared with a tape recorder and Miss Billie Tucker, president of Bubba's North Texas fan club. She'd brought along a list she'd compiled of characteristics Bubba and Elvis had in common. The disc jockey held up his microphone and she read it, perspiration on her upper lip.

"Both Elvis and Bubba are Capricorns," she said. "Both were truck drivers, both stationed with the army in Germany, and both were devoted to their mothers. Both are overweight, both like Cadillac Eldorados, and both like to stay up all night. Both have fantastic sex appeal . . ."

Good Lord, I thought. These people are serious.

Upstairs, I found myself in an ordinary high school auditorium. There were flags of the United States and Texas on either side of the stage. The ceiling was high, yellowish globes shedding a dim light. Probably the Pledge of Allegiance had been said here thousands of times. Tonight it was full of more middle-aged women than I'd ever seen in one place, and the clicking of high heels and pocketbooks was a constant roar.

Then the house lights went down and it got dead silent. The curtain rose in the darkness and a spotlight stabbed down and my brother leaped into it. He tore into "Heartbreak Hotel" like a man possessed. My brother, who had been good, had gotten better. Maybe he really was the best. He had all the moves down, and from this distance it made no difference at all that he wasn't a carbon copy of Elvis.

He sang "Blue Suede Shoes" and "Don't Be Cruel" and "Jailhouse Rock" and spoke of the series of miracles that had brought Elvis to the top in so short a time. He said Elvis had loved black music and made a plea for integration and sang "In the Ghetto." All this time, he was throwing scarves into the audience and women were fighting for them. Then he said, "There's been a great loss of faith in this country. Maybe it was Nixon, maybe Vietnam. I voted for Nixon, but he betrayed us. He thought he could get away with fooling us rednecks." He looked around, his face incandescent in the spotlight. "That's right. I'm a redneck. So are you. And so was Elvis. We're the people who kept the faith."

There was more, but I don't really remember all he said; and he didn't write it down, he spoke right from the heart. He asked for a moment of silence for the boys who had died in Vietnam, and sang "How Great Thou Art." Then he ripped right into "Hound Dog" and disappeared without an encore. The lights came up and we were back in that shabby little auditorium with flags on either side of the stage.

The audience went wild, like they'd just woke up, and I ran downstairs to Bubba's dressing room, where you could hear them stomping on the floor overhead.

Then Floyd said, "Here come the autograph hounds," and opened the door and they poured in. Bubba signed his own glossies as fast as they could shove them at him, and pretty soon a woman grabbed his gold chain and tore it right off his neck.

"We'd better get out of here, Bubba," Floyd said, and we shoved through the crowd. But they had our way blocked and we had to detour into the girls' rest room. Bubba was still laughing, but to tell the truth I was scared. We climbed out the window and ran across the parking lot, where someone from the band was waiting in the Eldorado. We all piled in and drove off, a crowd of women following us all the way to the corner.

"They shoulda had cops there," Bubba said after a while. "I told them we'd need cops. Floyd, you'd better start packing a rod. You're gonna need it if there's any more crowd scenes like this."

At Six Flags, Bubba demolished the other Elvis impersonators. What surprised me was how many there were. They came in all shapes and sizes, and one had come from as far away as Nebraska. There was only one who was serious competition: Claude Thibodeaux, from New Iberia, Louisiana, who billed himself as the Cajun Elvis. He had flash, but nobody could beat Bubba for sheer impact.

Right after his performance, Bubba was approached by someone who wanted to manage him. Elvis Presley's manager, as everyone knows, was Colonel Tom Parker. This was Bud Parker, late a colonel in the U.S. Air Force. The coincidence tickled them both. He promised Bubba in one year he'd be playing Caesar's Palace in Las Vegas.

I was packing my suitcase when Bubba came into my room and said, "Big brother, you and me are going to Houston."

"What for?"

"Looka here at this telegram."

The telegram was from Nancy Jo Miller, who'd been Bubba's high school love. She was married now and lived in Houston. She said she'd read about his act, congratulated him, and hoped they could get together sometime.

Sometimes my brother dumbfounded me. But I couldn't say no, and anyway, he was paying for the tickets. So instead of going home, we flew to Houston on Trans Texas, got a rented car and a room at the Holiday Inn.

Nancy Jo lived in a $200,000 brick colonial on the edge of Houston, with pine trees growing in the front yard. Bubba had this idea he wanted to drop in and surprise her, so we didn't phone ahead. He slipped on his shades and I rang the doorbell. I felt sorry for Bubba: He was as nervous as a kid on his first date.

Just for a moment I saw Nancy Jo as she really was, a little faded around the eyes and mouth. But the years had been good to her. I suppose you could say she resembled Angie Dickinson—which, in a way, was a hell of a lot better than she'd looked in high school.

"Oh, my Lord," she said, when she saw Bubba in his white Elvis jump suit, and gave a short, embarrassed laugh that was cut off as if by a knife. Then she said, "I'll make y'all bloody marys," and disappeared into the kitchen.

"This was a mistake," Bubba said. He was trembling so hard I had to hold him up.

Nancy Jo came back and we sat in the tiny front room with the big picture window, which I knew was almost never used except for guests. What with the baby grand piano and the big sofa and the glass-topped coffee table, there was hardly room for the three of us; but from the first, I don't even think they knew I was there. They were totally absorbed in each other. She poured out the story of all that had happened since they'd seen each other last, and I stared at the celery stalk in my bloody mary and tried not to listen.

Nancy Jo had intended to marry Bubba, but he had to do his army service, and there seemed to be all the time in the world; so she went to Dallas and enrolled in stewardess school. She pictured herself wearing that cute uniform and doing favors for the passengers, bringing them pillows and playing with their kids.

She lived with some other stews on Gaston Avenue, and there were some pretty wild parties; but Nancy Jo locked herself in her room and did crossword puzzles and wrote love letters to Bubba.

It was the airplane that did her in. The other stews hung out in the galley, where you could meet pro football players and rich oilmen. Nancy Jo didn't want a rich oilman: She was going to have Bubba. So she fought it.

But the airplane was the most boring place in the world. The kids were snotty and their parents were cross and didn't appreciate the favors you did for them. There was nothing to do but look out the window, and when you did, what did you see? Clouds.

In the end, she went to the galley, which was like a nickel-plated singles bar, so tiny you couldn't turn around without bumping into some horny guy. There she met Calvin Sloate, a corporate lawyer for Texaco; and they drank Scotch out of tiny bottles while the galley roared like a sea shell, rocking slightly in the rough air 20,000 feet over Indianapolis.

"I'm sorry, Bubba," she said. "But you were going to be in the army for another year and that seemed like forever. I had to get off that airplane." So she had married Calvin, and now seventeen years had flashed by like nothing at all.

"We've got a condo in Vero," she said, "and one in

14

Aspen, and last year we went skiing at Sundance and Lisa had her picture taken with Robert Redford."

"Lisa?" Bubba asked in a flat voice.

"My daughter," she said, showing us another picture. "That's her with her Arabian stallion. She loves horses."

She showed us the rest of the house. We stood for a moment at the door of Calvin's study, like visitors at a museum looking into one of those rooms closed off with a velvet rope. Calvin had a collection of beer cans, one from every country in the world; a pair of expensive shotguns; and a lampshade made of *Playboy* centerfolds. I had already noticed his radar-equipped bass boat in the driveway.

In the bedroom, she slid back the closet door and showed us her $500 Italian shoes. Bubba just looked at her and said, "You know you broke my heart, don't you?"

"Oh, Bubba, don't say that. It sounds so horrible. And, anyway, how could I know you cared that much? Look here."

She took from under her costly shoes the old high school yearbook; and there, on the same page, were their pictures. Their faces were soft and unformed but shining with a sort of light. Bubba had a flattop with "fenders" —long on the sides and short on the top. Over his face he had written, in blue ballpoint pen: "Had a lot of good times with you and hope to see more of you next year. Bubba."

"Couldn't you have said more than that?" she asked, tears in her eyes. "How was I to know I was so important to you?"

"In those days," Bubba said, "you won the game of love by pretending you didn't care. Yeah, that's all we thought love was, a game. But it turned out to be a more serious game than we thought."

At this point I left the room, phoned a cab, and went back to the Holiday Inn. I don't think they missed me. It rained, and there I spent the rest of the afternoon watching *Return to Earth*, a TV movie about the life of an astronaut, and drinking Jack Daniel's. Later, Bubba came back. "Well, big brother," he said, "it's all settled. She's leaving her husband and I'm leaving my wife, and everything's going to be like it was." He'd been walking around in the rain and his clothes were soaked.

But I was skeptical that Bubba could so easily turn back the clock. Now that he'd become a star, he thought anything was possible. To me, he was like that astronaut who'd achieved his boyhood dream and went to the moon; but sooner or later, he had to come back down to earth and be an ordinary person like the rest of us. On the plane home, Bubba turned to me and said, "Big brother, I'm going to tell you something. You're the only one who'll understand."

"Yes, Bubba?"

"My whole life, I've felt like I was in the wrong body or something. But when I'm Elvis . . . I got it right. I'm the person I should have been, the person I've always known I could be."

Now it struck me that this was what Bobby Joe Pitts, the would-be transsexual, had said. Like Bubba, he only felt like himself when he was somebody else.

"Do you know what I'm saying?" Bubba whispered, holding my shoulder in an iron grip.

Yes, I knew. At the best moments of my life—when I hit a good golf shot or had a woman I adored—I felt like someone else. A version of me, maybe, but a version that was to Ross Moody what a Cadillac Eldorado was to a

Ford Pinto. I doubted you could totally become that perfect version of yourself. Bubba felt that way now, but he could not be El Tex As for the rest of his life.

But that was the happiest I ever saw Bubba. On this flight, we had, instead of a stewardess, a male flight attendant. Ordinarily, Bubba would have made some sarcastic comment; but on that day, he seemed at peace with himself. I slept most of the way, but once I woke up. Bubba, in the hollow roar of the cabin, was looking through the porthole and smiling down at the dark world below.

When he broke the news to his wife, Jan, she knew just how to take it: like Jill Clayburgh in that movie about the New York woman, nodding, her eyes closed, finishing his sentences for him.

"And so," he said, "I am going to—"

"Move out. All right, buster, go ahead. Do yourself a big favor."

They were standing in the den, and she poked through the big glass bowl on top of the television set full of matchbooks from every restaurant they'd ever been to.

"You'd just better get yourself a good lawyer," she told him.

The strange thing, he said, was that she seemed almost glad. Here it was, the crisis predicted so often. Now she would learn to think for herself and be happy (like Rhoda once she got rid of that slob, Joe), maybe even write a book. The possibilities were endless.

"There is one more thing," Bubba said. "Here is a list of our close friends whom I do not want you to sleep with, as they would be laughing at me behind my back."

"Thank you," she said. "I know just what to do with it."

She slept with the first one, Bubba's boss at the Prudential, that very night; and spent the rest of the week working her way down the list.

Nancy Jo also left Calvin Sloate but, on the advice of a girlfriend, went to a therapist, and the first thing he did was tell her not to make any more sudden moves.

She phoned Bubba and said, "I'm living in an apartment complex with plastic ivy on the walls. There's nobody here but kids; and my lawyer says I won't get any kind of settlement, since I moved out. Bubba, I'm having second thoughts."

So Bubba sped down to Houston, even though he was starting another tour in a few days. Nancy Jo wouldn't see him right away: She had to look through her appointment book and set a date. When they finally got together, all she would do was talk for hours. She had a whole new vocabulary and she wouldn't drink bloody marys anymore, just white wine and something called Amaretto, which Bubba said tasted like Log Cabin syrup.

She was changing, slipping away; but Bubba was desperate to prove he could accept her under any conditions. He went to see her therapist himself and even took her to a Woody Allen movie.

I didn't see Bubba for months. At the end of his tour, he phoned from Abilene and asked if I'd come down. I found him that night at the Cross Plains Motel, a real dump.

His appearance shocked me: He'd gained maybe forty pounds. He said, "Did you bring your little black bag?"

"Yeah. What for?"

"You got any speed in it?"

I was offended and told him to forget it. He said it was hard for him to keep his weight down, being on the road and all and eating nothing but junk food. But I wouldn't be talked into it. Then I went right into the john and flushed all my pills down the toilet.

When I came back out, Bubba was talking to Floyd, who had his hair dyed red. I sat down and noticed my chair had a Rocking R brand on the arm. It was Roy Rogers furniture, probably bought for some kid thirty years ago, and it had ended up here in this terrible motel. For the first time, I glimpsed the sadness singers talk about of being on the road, and thought it was getting to Bubba.

Floyd said he had a girl for Bubba. "Tell her I'll meet her in one hour," Bubba said. "The usual conditions."

The conditions under which Bubba met his fans were these: They had to be between the ages of thirty-five and forty-five, they had to provide their own car, and they had to park on a dirt road on the edge of town. When Bubba appeared in the Eldorado, they flashed their lights if it was safe. Then Bubba parked and came ahead on foot, bringing his own bottle.

I thought this was a foolish, adolescent thing to do, and told him so.

"You know, big brother," he said, "I feel sorry for you. You been fooling around with women's private parts for so long you've forgotten what they're for."

Like everything Bubba said, there was some truth to this. In my years as a gynecologist, I'd examined most of the girls I'd worshipped in high school, and it meant less than nothing to me. It made me wonder about my choice of profession.

"When are you playing Las Vegas?" I asked him.

"Colonel Parker says I'm not ready for Vegas. I need one more thing to put me over the top—plastic surgery, so I'm identical to Elvis. 'Course, there'll be no goin' back— but it's worth it if it gets me to Caesar's Palace."

19

"No," I said. "No, Bubba. You can't do that."

"Why not?"

I couldn't exactly say, but I was thinking: If he loses his face, he loses himself.

"Bobby Joe Pitts decided not to," I said.

"Bobby Joe Pitts?"

"You know. The plastic surgeon told him he should try living like a woman. Well he joined a women's group, and now he's changed his mind. He says he thought men were boring, but women have the most boring conversations in the world."

This got my brother furious. "Are you comparing me to some miserable little pervert? Christ, Bobby Joe . . . why, he wore a brassiere under his football jersey the whole senior year. And we thought he was joking!"

"Will Nancy Jo love you if you don't have your own face?"

He took a pistol out of the desk drawer, a Colt Python, and spun it around his finger and said, "Nancy Jo doesn't know what she wants. Last time I talked to her, she said she wanted space. I said, 'Hell, you can have all the space you want, once we're married.' " He aimed the pistol at the television screen, where Elvis was singing to Ann-Margret. It was a reshowing of *Viva Las Vegas* on cable TV.

"His voice sorta went to pieces, didn't it?" Bubba said. "Frankly, I think I'm better now than he ever was."

"Bubba, put down that gun."

"Come on," he said. "I'm going to get some nooky."

So Floyd drove us out to the edge of town, where we parked on a dirt road and could see ahead, dimly, the outline of another car.

"She's not flashing her lights," Floyd said. "It must not be safe yet."

20

I rolled down the window. There was a full moon that night and I thought I could hear the distant yip of coyotes.

When I mentioned it, Floyd said, "Ain't no more coyotes in this county. Farmers wiped them out with traps and poisoned bait."

Still, I thought I could hear them, as I had on so many nights when we'd driven out on Red River Road.

"Do you have to do this, Bubba? What about Nancy Jo?"

"A man's got to get his satisfaction. And if you can't be near the one you love, love the one you're near."

The headlights of the other car flashed.

Bubba opened the door.

"Don't go, Bubba."

"You know, big brother," he said, "you ought to come with me. It would do you good to see how those ladies give me all that good X-rated sex they been holding out on their husbands all these years." He came around and opened my door. "Just stand outside and listen. She won't mind. Thrill to the days of yesteryear, big brother. Come along with me and I'll show you how good that low-rent lovin' can still be."

And, God help me, I did. My heart was pounding, but I stepped out of the car and followed my brother down the road in the moonlight.

"You know, Bubba, you are a devil. You have the damnedest way of getting people to do what you want."

"Don't I know it?"

"You were right about me being a gynecologist and all. Somehow, I lost interest in women. It just slipped away from me like everything else."

"The things closest to you go first," he said. "They

21

slip away so softly you don't notice. You wake up one morning the stranger in a strange land."

"You're right," I said. "But women are . . . everything."

"Yea, verily, good buddy."

"Sex may be the secret of American life. In fact, I see now . . ."

But I don't know what I saw, for what happened next drove everything out of my head. The headlights of the car came on, blinding us, and we heard a male voice say, "Try to screw my wife, will you, you sons of bitches! I'll kill you!" Then a shotgun went off and I heard the shot rip through the air right over our heads. The car was rolling toward us and Bubba and I were running back down the road.

"The fence, big brother," Bubba shouted, "hit for the fence." And I dove under it, the barbed wire tearing the coat right off my back. Then we were stumbling through the prickly pear, the shotgun still going off and one pellet stinging the back of my neck like a yellow jacket.

Bubba grabbed me and threw me down. The car stopped and a spotlight probed around until it found us. Bubba leaped up, his fists balled, a foolhardy, magnificent sight. I thought: This is the end of your life, Ross.

Then we heard Floyd laughing and barking like a dog. "Come out, come out, wherever you are, Elvis."

It was all a big joke.

Bubba picked up a clod and threw it at the car, but Floyd only laughed harder. The band had been in on it—I could hear them laughing, too. My face was scratched and my palms were full of cactus thorns, and I could feel cold air on my back where my jacket had been ripped off.

Bubba climbed over the fence and threw himself at Floyd. They circled in the headlights, Bubba throwing wild punches and Floyd dodging them, shouting, "Shitfire and save matches, Bubba. Can't you take a joke?"

"Joke! We coulda been hurt running around in that goddamned cactus patch."

"Oh, hell, you're just pissed off 'cause we pulled that same trick on you in high school. I never thought you'd be stupid enough to fall for it twice."

That stopped Bubba. "All right," he said. "So I did. But this time it wasn't funny. We're grown men now, not high school kids."

Floyd kept laughing.

"All right, Floyd, you're fired. That's right. I'm giving you notice."

Somebody from the band stepped forward and said he thought Bubba was being too harsh, and Bubba fired him, too. He looked around and said, "Anybody else?"

Then everybody said it was fine with them; they were getting fed up with Bubba, anyway. There were some bitter words. It ended up with us going back to the motel and them going off to a honky-tonk to get drunk.

On the way back, Bubba began wondering where he was going to get another band. His troubles were multiplying and he said, "Maybe I should just shoot myself."

"Don't talk that way, Bubba."

At the motel, the television was still on, nothing showing on the screen now but snow. I went into the bathroom, threw my torn jacket in the trash can, and started putting iodine on the scratches on my face. The shot lifted me right off the floor.

He was sitting on the bed, holding the pistol. The television was exploded, a bullet through the picture tube. "I always wanted to know how he felt when he did that," Bubba said. "Now I know."

*　　*　　*

23

Things went downhill fast after that. My brother never found another band. The bookings dried up and Colonel Parker lost interest. The IRS was now investigating Bubba's income taxes, and in the middle of it all he got a Dear John letter from Nancy Jo saying she'd fallen in love with her psychiatrist.

He went down to Houston with the idea of confronting her but, instead, went to Calvin Sloate's house. Calvin himself answered the door and Bubba said, "I'm the son of a bitch who ran off with your wife."

"I know," Calvin said. "You're Bubba Moody. Come on in and let's let it all hang out."

Bubba, feeling numb all over, walked into Lisa's room. She was lying on her bed under a John Travolta poster.

"Your mother doesn't love me anymore," he said.

"I know. I think she's making a big mistake."

"You're the closest thing to her, the way she once was," Bubba said. "You're beautiful."

"Thanks, Bubba. I like your looks, too."

"Will you marry me?"

"Are you serious?"

"Dead serious," he said, and kissed her on her teenage lips.

When he turned around, Calvin was standing in the door.

Bubba phoned from Houston and said he'd been shot in the leg. It was nothing serious—Calvin had used a .22 target pistol. Before I left, I went over to tell Jan, who'd just gotten back from a trip to Las Vegas with Harley Otis. When I got there, she was gluing silver dollars to the top of the coffee table.

"Look here at all the money I won," she said. "Seems like my luck just won't quit."

When she heard about Bubba, she said, "That's his problem. All that's behind me now. I'm starting over."

She disappeared into the kitchen and I was left alone with the television. Tom Snyder was interviewing a judge in California who'd started divorcing fifty people in a group. There were no lawyers required, he just asked everyone if they had irreconcilable differences. When they said they did, he pronounced them divorced and they headed for the door. The men moved slowly, but the women were smiling and hopeful, and I thought how much better women seemed to adjust to modern life. "So would you say this is . . . the coming thing?" Tom Snyder asked, and the judge said it was.

"Notice anything different?" she said, coming back into the room.

"No. Is your hair shorter?"

She told me she'd had silicone injections. "Come on, Ross, you know my breasts always drooped."

"No, Jan. I've never noticed."

She put down her glass of white wine and lay on the floor. "See? They're nice and hard. They're the same standing up or laying down. They're just like doorknobs."

"I honestly can't tell the difference, Jan."

She leaned so close I could feel her breath on my cheek. "Go ahead and put your hand on them. I don't mind. Feel the difference for yourself."

I excused myself and drove home, the whole side of my face burning like I'd stood too close to a hot stove.

So Bubba never got his plastic surgery or a trip to Las Vegas (although his wife did). He ended up driving a truck again, but to me he seemed happier, and I found I enjoyed knowing him more than I had since we were kids. He still, however, had his problems with the IRS,

25

and one night, in the dead of that winter, he tapped on my patio doors. We sat outside, in the darkness, while my wife watched *Family Feud*. (She seemed to draw strength from that program: She never missed it.)

"The government lawyers are coming Monday," Bubba said, "and I'm liable to do a couple of years in prison."

I told him I'd lend him money, but he said after the divorce he couldn't face going to court again.

"Let's take one last ride out Red River Road," he said, "in case I never see it again."

So we took a six-pack and drove out and parked on the edge of town, where the pumping jacks rose and fell in the fields on either side.

"You know," he said, "Elvis himself couldn't make it today. Everything today glorifies the loser, the person who can't help himself. Someone like me doesn't stand a chance. Yeah, it's the decade of the loser; and it's the losers who did me in. Come on, big brother, let's go ride those pumping jacks."

So we did. He could always talk me into anything. He sat on one end and I on the other, hanging on for dear life, and we rose and fell like two kids on a gigantic seesaw.

"Well, if that's the way this country's going to be," he shouted over the roar of the diesel, "they can have it. I want no part of it. I'll go right on, trying to do the impossible. Look, big brother," he said, reaching over his head as the pumping jack rose, "I can touch the moon."

Then he fell off. I thought he was dead. But he groaned and threw up in the weeds, and I cleaned him off as best I could.

"We'd better go home, Bubba," I said.

"He never died," Bubba said. "Not really."

"He did die, Bubba. Of a heart attack. We've all got to get older and die."

"No, big brother. I'll let you in on a secret. You and I are going to be the first people in history who don't."

The men from the IRS came on Monday, but Bubba was gone. Floyd, who was now back with the highway patrol, found his truck parked by the side of the road near Electra. There'd been lots of UFO sightings the night before. A farmer near Bowie found his cows dead, emptied out; nothing left of them but horns, hooves, and hide, and not a drop of blood on the ground, either. The lights of Bubba's truck were still on, and his CB radio, the key turned to SEND. Floyd found one footprint in the sandy soil just the other side of the fence, apparently headed for a strange depression in the ground, where all the grass was dead. It made the front page of the papers, and the sermon that Sunday was "A Close Encounter with Your God."

Then things got more or less back to normal here in Nortex. Bobby Joe Pitts started a marriage counseling service. He saw himself as someone who'd known the problem from both sides, a sort of Kissinger in the war between the sexes. Harley Otis got a divorce and married Jan, but it wasn't long before she showed up at Stolen Hours, a new bar for housewives where they could drink all afternoon, watch the soaps, and perhaps have a casual affair. Floyd forgot his grudge against Bubba and we spent several nights talking about all that had happened. "I'll tell you one thing," he said. "Your brother was the most remarkable person ever born around here."

In October, I finally made love to Nadine MacAfee. But we both discovered that what we had looked forward to for so long took only moments to do, and naturally this was a disappointment. We parted friends, but it confirmed my idea that the past is a closed book: You don't tamper with it.

But that night I couldn't sleep, and long after they played the national anthem on television, and showed the airplane and the prayer, I was still pacing the floor and feeling like a ghost. Then the phone rang.

"Hello, big brother."

For a moment I couldn't see or speak. "I just wanted to let you know," Bubba said, "I'm still on the planet Earth. In fact, I'm in Globe, Arizona."

"It's good to hear your voice, Bubba."

"It's good to hear yours. Hey, this is great country out here. Leaving that town was the best thing I ever did." He told me he was working as a disc jockey, but he had big plans. There was an old abandoned drive-in out on the edge of town, and he was going to renovate it and call it Bubba's Fifties Burger.

"You know," he said. "Carhops on roller skates, neon lights, and on the jukebox some of that great old rock and roll."

"Better keep a low profile, Bubba. You're still a wanted man."

"Don't worry about that," he said. "The road's right out my back door. And if I have to split, well, that won't be so bad either. If there's a prettier sight than an American blacktop road goin' nowhere in the moonlight, I don't know what it is."

There was a click, then nothing but echoes along one thousand miles of telephone cable.

Well, goddamn. I took three or four shots of Jack Daniel's and did a sort of dance out there on my patio, hopping around under the stars. Then I got in the car to go tell Floyd the good news: that the King was still with us.

BOOM TOWN

Bobby stood atop a hill, the setting sun at his back, and stared at his shadow, which fell across other hills, all covered with short yellow grass, rolling away as far as the eye could see. In the remote distance were toylike oil rigs, and on the very horizon, the lights of Gillette, Wyoming.

Three months ago he had been back in Nortex, just out of high school, living with his mother. Then one night his Uncle Mickey had shown up.

Mickey was the drifter of the family. Every other year he'd disappear for several months and come back with a million funny stories about working on a pipeline or an offshore platform. He'd told Bobby's mother he was going to Gillette for the big energy boom, and offered to take Bobby along. They could make big coin roughnecking on an oil rig, and the boy could learn a little about real life.

That was an expression Mickey used often, *big coin*, and it had sounded good to Bobby, who'd been working for Montgomery Ward.

So they'd driven up in Mickey's old Ford pickup, Bobby learning lots of things, like how to siphon gas with a length of rubber hose that Mickey called an Oklahoma Credit Card. And all the way, Mickey had kept saying how great it was going to be, telling Bobby he was going to teach him how to play world-class poker, promising to introduce him to some boom town women who would teach him things those Church of Christ girls in Nortex never could.

But things hadn't turned out the way Mickey had promised. For one thing, ten thousand other guys had gotten the idea first. Gillette was impossibly crowded, and impossibly expensive. Rooms cost fifty dollars a night. There were only about ten or fifteen girls in the whole town, and the ones Bobby had tried to talk to had ignored him completely. They'd finally gotten jobs roughnecking, but they were spending their coin as fast as they could make it, and had to resort to desperate measures just to stay alive. For one three-day period, they'd both lived on a single Slim Jim.

Just thinking about it made Bobby hungry. When the sun went down, he turned and walked back across the top of the hill. Fifty yards away, Mickey's old Ford was parked. Next to it was a couch, an easy chair, a standing lamp, and an icebox. Mickey was sitting on the couch. He had plugged in the lamp and was reading in a little pool of light.

This was another one of Mickey's ideas—living out here on the prairie. One day they'd been out driving around, and Mickey had opened a gate and had driven up to the top of this hill. "Why should we go back to that town," he'd asked, "where we've got to spend all our coin just keeping a roof over our heads? Why not set up housekeeping right here?"

Bobby had protested that this land belonged to somebody. It was somebody else's property.

"Sure, it belongs to somebody," Mickey had said. "He's only got about a million acres. Don't you think he can afford to spare us some room?"

So they'd bought the furniture from the Salvation Army, and the icebox, and the three big Delco batteries they used for power. The hill couldn't be seen from the road, and so far nobody seemed to know they were there. The couch folded out into a bed. On cool nights, they slept under a Space Blanket. At least they weren't starving to death, and Mickey said it wouldn't rain for a couple of months yet.

But Bobby had the feeling they just couldn't get away with this. It was too easy. Sometimes he woke up in the middle of the night and found a Hereford staring at him in the moonlight, its sad eyes full of what looked like disapproval.

He got a package of cookies out of the icebox and opened a beer. "What are you reading?" he asked Mickey.

Mickey looked up. The bristles of his beard stood out white against his sunburned skin. But he was pretty fit for a guy who was pushing forty.

"I'm reading about those big salmon up in Alaska," he said. "Do you know there's a time of year in Alaska when the salmon are so thick all you got to do is throw in a hook and pull 'em out?"

Mickey was always talking about Alaska; saying when he made his pile he was going to go up there and make a down payment on a fishing boat. Fishing, Mickey said, wasn't work. It was pure pleasure.

31

"I don't believe it," Bobby said. "Nothing's that easy."

Mickey put down his magazine. "Feeling poorly?"

"I guess I'm homesick."

Mickey laughed. "Go on back to Texas and work for Monkey Ward's, if that's what you want. But I'm staying. This is my chance to make big coin, and I ain't leaving until I do."

Bobby pointed out to Mickey that they weren't exactly making big coin.

"We got our freedom, son," Mickey said. "That's the important thing. This is a lot better than living in the city."

"Yeah, we got our freedom," Bobby said. "But sometimes when that sun goes down, I get to feeling real lonesome."

"Write your mom a letter."

"It's not my mom I miss."

Mickey looked thoughtful. "A healthy young man like you needs female companionship," he said. "I should have thought of this before."

"Yeah," Bobby said, "but all those girls in Gillette care about is coin, and I ain't got it. You can't get something for nothing, Mickey," he said. "You just can't. And if I don't find a girl pretty soon, I'm going home."

"Why, I'll get you a girl," Mickey said. "And you won't have to spend a nickel."

He rolled a cigarette, and Bobby found himself listening, even though he didn't think there was a way in the world Mickey could do that.

"It's true," Mickey said, "we never got anyplace with those girls in Gillette. They were too spoiled to see our true worth. What we've got to do is find some girls who are so far down even we look good to them. And I think I know where to look."

"Where?"

Mickey scratched a match with his thumbnail and lit his cigarette. "Jail."

"You mean we've got to go to jail?"

"Of course not," Mickey said. "All we've got to do is hang around the local jail, and hit on the first two ladies who come out."

The more Bobby thought, the more he could see what Mickey was getting at. There were probably girls in that jail who were starved for affection. Girls who hadn't had their hands on a man in months.

"Uncle Mickey," he said. "You just may have come up with a great idea."

On their next day off, they shaved, put on clean shirts, and drove into Gillette. They parked across from the jail, and it wasn't an hour before two girls came out.

One was blonde, the other dark. They wore sunglasses, tube tops, and leather boots.

"Hookers," Mickey said. "Do you care?"

"Doesn't bother me," Bobby said.

Mickey got out and crossed the street. Bobby stayed in the car and watched him talking to the girls. He'd learned Mickey could talk anyone into anything. Pretty soon he came back with the girls and they got in the car.

"I'm Brenda," the dark-haired older one said, "and this is Cathy."

They were a lot better looking than he'd expected. In fact, they looked as good as any girls he'd ever seen back home in Nortex.

"Where are we gonna eat?" Brenda said.

"I promised these girls a meal," Mickey said. "What say we go out to our place?"

On the way, the girls told them their story. They usually worked truckstops and rodeos. Somebody had told them there was big coin to be made in Gillette, but they'd had some pretty disappointing experiences. They'd gotten busted three days after they'd arrived, and the judge had given them thirty days. "You got a real low class of customer here, too," Brenda said.

"You sure do," Cathy said. "After this, I'm going into telephone sex."

Then they pulled off the highway and drove up the little dirt road to the hilltop. The girls were a little surprised when they saw nothing but loose furniture.

"Where's your house?" Brenda said.

"I don't think we ever mentioned a house," Mickey said. "And you've got to admit, the view is spectacular."

They looked at each other. "Maybe we should go," Cathy said.

"Oh, what the hell," Brenda said. "I'm so glad to get out of that jail I don't much care. Would you boys be looking for a good time tonight?"

"You don't understand," Mickey said. "No money's gonna change hands tonight. That would just spoil it."

He opened a bottle of Austin Nichols's Wild Turkey, his favorite bourbon, and poured everyone a stiff drink.

"As we see it, you've been wronged by society. You ain't criminals. You practice the oldest art in the world— the art of love. And what could be wrong with that?"

Brenda looked at Cathy and said, "This guy is *cool*."

"You ladies got a dirty deal," Mickey went on, "and tonight we're gonna make it up to you. We offer you good food, good drinks, and some pleasant conversation. If things go beyond that, fine. But you're under no obligation to perform."

Bobby couldn't believe the girls would go for such a line of bullshit, but they did, especially when Mickey fired up the Hibachi and took four big sirloin steaks out of

34

the icebox. It helped that for the last month they hadn't had anything to eat but baloney sandwiches. When the steaks were ready they gobbled them right down. Bobby had never seen girls eat like that before. In five minutes, there was nothing left but bones.

Then Mickey poured another round of drinks and said it was time to watch the sun go down. "Watching the sun go down is the big entertainment around here," he said. "When it's real good, we applaud."

By now the girls were getting pretty friendly. Bobby was thinking maybe things could work out just as easy as Mickey said they could. Cathy was sitting on the couch. He figured it was time to put a move on her, so he sat down next to her.

"You work out at the strip mine?" she asked him.

"We're roughnecks," he told her. "We came here from Texas."

Cathy told him she'd met Brenda in Billings, and they'd decided to stick together because things were easier if you had a friend. Just like me and Mickey, he thought.

"We're hoping to make enough to buy a condo in Vail," she said. "But so far, we ain't made a nickel."

"We ain't made that much either," Bobby admitted.

Mickey and Brenda were sitting on the ground, passing the bottle back and forth.

"You don't really believe all those things you were saying, do you?" she asked him.

"Why, of course I do," Mickey said. "I got a lot of respect for you ladies. Now, you take those girls in Gillette. They're selling it—they're just not out front about it, like you are."

He poured himself another drink. "And you're probably very good at what you do, while most of them ain't."

"Yeah," Cathy said. "But most guys don't appreciate that. They want you to tell them how good they are. They think paying for it's the important thing."

"That's what's wrong with America today," Mickey said. "People worship the almighty coin instead of respecting someone for what they do well. Why, back in the days of ancient Greece and Rome, people who practiced the art of love were celebrities. They had great respect."

Bobby was lost in admiration for Mickey's bullshit. The more he drank, the better it got.

"You know," Brenda said to Mickey, "you sorta remind me of my husband."

"You tried it too?"

"Sure," she said. "Lived in a mobile home in Billings. That's when I was your everyday housewife. Dyed my hair seven different shades of blonde, and he always had a beer in his hand. The neighbors called us Lord Budweiser and Lady Clairol."

"I've got nothing against marriage in theory," Mickey said, "except it's a life without hope. When you're married, you've got to have coin. Oh, I tried. But every night I'd lie awake thinking, I don't know how much longer I can stand this. I had only one hope."

"What was that?"

"Publisher's Clearing House," he said. "I told my wife to mail every goddamned one of those things in."

Then Mickey stood up, his drink in his hand, and looked at the setting sun. "I'd rather live out here, on nothing." He smiled at Brenda. "We're the last of the free men. And you ladies are the last of the free women."

They just sat there for a little while, feeling the bourbon, listening to nothing, just the silence that was broken now and then by a bird singing somewhere you couldn't even see. Then the sun touched the horizon, and Mickey started clapping, as hard as he could. "Bravo, God," Mickey yelled. "Primo." Everybody joined in.

Mickey got out his Merle Haggard records, plugged in the record player, and asked Brenda to dance. Bobby watched them moving in slow circles. By now the sun was gone, leaving a yellow glow in the sky, like the light from a blast furnace, and a million stars had started to appear.

Cathy looked up at the night sky and sighed. "Just look at those stars," she said. "You guys have got the right idea, living out here like this."

Bobby nodded. He knew he should ask her to dance, but for some reason he couldn't. It was a beautiful night. The sky looked like one of those paintings on velvet, but with grains of salt scattered here and there for stars.

"And look over there," she said, taking his hand. "You can see the lights of Gillette. Looks like you could reach right out and touch 'em."

Bobby wanted to tell her how he'd felt out here, on all those nights when the sun had gone down and he'd stared off fifty miles at those lights. Everything was so far apart out here it made you feel like nothing.

"I don't know," he said. "Sometimes I look at those lights, and I feel like there's some kind of party going on, and I should be there. I want to *be* somebody," he said. "How's anybody gonna know who I am so long as I'm stuck out here?"

"I know just what you mean," she said.

"Do you?"

"When I'm out in the country," she said, "looking up at the stars like this, I'm always hoping I'll see a UFO. Then somebody could write an article about me for the *National Enquirer.*"

It wasn't exactly what he'd meant, but it was close enough. He put his arm around her, wondering what would happen when he got this girl alone.

Mickey and Brenda were dancing slower and slower. She was whispering in his ear.

"I told you," he heard Mickey say. "No money's gonna change hands tonight."

"This one's on the house," she said. "And you're really gonna like it."

Mickey picked up the Space Blanket and said to Bobby, "I guess we'll be going for a walk. You keep the home fires burning now, you hear?"

"Sure, Hoss," Bobby said.

Mickey socked his arm and they disappeared into the darkness.

He turned to Cathy, who was staring into the fire in the Hibachi.

"What are you thinking?" he said.

"Your buddy's beautiful."

"Mickey?" he said. "But he's got all that gray hair. Why, he's almost forty years old."

"Yeah," she said. "But for an old dude, he's super cool."

"You wouldn't think so if you had to live with him." He got up and poured himself another drink, intensely disappointed.

"You know something?" Cathy said.

"What?"

"This sort of reminds me of a pamphlet a Jehovah's Witness gave me once," she said. "It said nuclear war was the Armageddon predicted in the Holy Bible. But after God had cleansed the world of sin with nuclear weapons, there was gonna be peace everywhere. And it showed these people living out in the country, just like you guys. And their children were playing with the bears and mountain lions, just like in *The Wilderness Family*."

He went back to the couch and sat down next to her. "You're not religious or something, are you?"

"I used to be," she said. "My parents were footwashing Pentecostal Baptists. But all the Bible stories gave me impure thoughts." She stopped and stared into the fire for a minute. Then she said, "There was this boy named Rodney who went to our church. He had long, blonde hair and this sick, suffering look, just like Jesus Christ himself."

"What happened?" Bobby said.

"One night I washed his feet and dried them with my hair, just like the women in the Scriptures. Then he made me holler for the love of the Lord."

Bobby thought this was one of the most interesting stories he'd ever heard. His heart was pounding. It's now or never, he thought, and pressed his lips to hers.

"Cathy," he said. "There's something you could do that would make me so happy."

"Bobby," she said. "Let's don't spoil it."

"Spoil it?"

"It's been so nice tonight," she said, "just being treated like a lady. All I've needed for so long was for somebody to make me feel like I'm worth something."

"Well, shit," he said. "*They're* doing it."

"They really like each other, can't you tell?"

"But you're a hooker. There've been so many guys. Would one more make any difference?"

"If that's the way you feel, Bobby," she said in an icy voice, "then I'm really disappointed in you."

Somehow he'd known from the beginning that tonight was not to be his night. It had been too much to hope for.

He felt a great tiredness creeping over him that made everything unimportant. "You're right," he said, putting his head on her shoulder. "Let's just hold hands."

Some time later there was a brilliant flash that he could see even through closed eyelids.

"What was that?" he said, leaping to his feet.

He looked around. The fire had burned down to glowing coals. He must have been asleep.

"I didn't see anything," she said. Then they heard the rumble of thunder. "It's going to storm."

"No it's not," he said. "It's not. Mickey had said it never rained this time of year." Then another flash of lightning lit the hilltop bright as day, and he saw big clouds rolling in from the north.

In the next flash, he saw Mickey running toward him, the Space Blanket wrapped around him. Then the wind hit, and Bobby's eyes were filled with blowing dust, and from that moment on his impressions were confused. He could see only in the flashes of lightning, but he could see well enough to make out everything blowing away. The lamp was already gone. So were the sheets. In another flash of lightning, he saw Mickey's records go flying past. Mickey was running around trying to hold everything down, but it was too late. Bobby saw the Space Blanket go flying off too, like a big piece of tinfoil. Then big drops of cold rain were hitting him in the face, and all he could hear above the roar of the storm was Mickey yelling, "Oh shit, oh shit," over and over.

Finally they gave up and joined the girls in the pickup, feeling it rock in the gusts of wind.

The girls couldn't stop laughing. "What's so god-damned funny?" Mickey wanted to know.

Bobby could hold his anger back no longer. "What's

so funny?" he shouted. "Why, we are. We were fools to think we could get away with this."

"What are you yelling at me for?" Mickey said. "I can't control the weather."

"It was a stupid idea in the first place. Ain't you never heard the story of the grasshopper and the ants? We were the grasshopper, fiddling in the sun. Now we're paying for it. We've lost everything we owned, and it's all your fault."

Mickey was completely naked except for his boxer shorts. He took a big drink from the bottle. "I didn't need all that shit anyway," he said.

"Well, what are we gonna do now?" Brenda asked.

"At least I've still got my ol' Ford," Mickey said. He turned the ignition key and the motor roared into life. "Let's go into town and raise some hell."

He drove down the hill and across the prairie. The girls were still laughing, but Bobby knew this was getting serious. When he got to the fence, Mickey put the gas pedal to the floor and drove right through it.

At that moment, Bobby knew he'd had enough of his Uncle Mickey. He wanted four walls and a steady job. He wished he'd stayed in Nortex and worked for Montgomery Ward. When they got back to Gillette, he'd phone his mother and ask her to send him the money for a bus ticket home.

They roared down the slippery road, the Ford jolting over ruts and stones that threatened to snap the axle. "Don't you think you're driving a little fast?" Brenda asked.

Mickey, one hand on the wheel, took a big gulp from the bottle. "Don't worry," he said. "I'm the greatest goddamned driver in the world."

PURE SEX

O n the coldest morning of
the year, David woke to
the sound of Audrey crying and brought her a bottle. Holding her in his arms, he looked out the window. For a week,
every day had been the same—cold and dry, with a
strong wind blowing from the north. The carpet was full
of static electricity; sparks shot from his fingertips when
he touched a doorknob or a light switch, with a loud,
painful snap.

Two months ago, his wife had been offered a job at
Channel 13. David, who was an actor, had told her to
take it. It was a good career move for her, and David
wanted to spend more time with Audrey. He had thought
he could easily perform all the duties of a parent and still
go to the auditions his agent thought were important. But
somehow there was never enough time. David found
himself falling into Audrey's schedule. When she slept, he
slept; when she woke, he hurried around the neighbor-

hood, trying to get everything done before his wife got home.

He looked at the list his wife had push-pinned to the bulletin board above her desk. Today he had to buy groceries and a bottle of white wine. Then he had to go to the apartment of the producer his wife worked for, who was out of town this week, and water his plants. He looked at the clock. It was almost noon. Time to get started.

David liked the cold: It made you careful, it made you think. He dressed Audrey in her snowsuit, strapped her into the Snugli on his chest, buttoning his down jacket around her so that her face was almost hidden in the billowing blue folds. Then he locked the several locks on his apartment door and rode the elevator down to the street.

They lived on the Upper West Side, between Broadway and the Hudson River. It was a neighborhood of old people: Even in this cold they were everywhere, pushing along in chrome walkers, their nurses following a few steps behind. David would have liked to have lived somewhere else, but his wife thought it was a good neighborhood to bring up children, and they could afford the rent. There were only a few young people on the streets—young mothers, who, like David, carried their children on their backs or across their chests.

When he had first started taking care of Audrey, David had thought he might get to know some of them—perhaps in the grocery store, where they could talk parent to parent. But his attempts to make conversation had failed. They didn't seem to want to talk to a man about taking care of children. He supposed they would rather be at work, like his wife; and found himself feeling sorry for them.

David had been to the grocery and was on his way to buy the bottle of wine when he saw Paula step out of a store up the street.

He stopped and looked into a store window, but she had already seen him.

"Hello, David," she said.

"What are you doing here?" he heard himself say.

"I came up here to meet somebody else," she said. "I wasn't looking for you."

He felt everyone was looking at her chopped-off blonde hair and black leather jacket. He felt everyone knew who they were and what they had meant to each other. Of course the people passing were total strangers, but that was how he felt.

"Do you want to see the baby?" he asked her. It was the only thing he could think of to say.

"Sure."

He pushed aside the folds of his jacket so that she could see Audrey's sleeping face.

"Do you think she looks like me?" he said.

"I don't know," Paula said. "She's a beautiful baby."

The wind gusted around them. It was too cold; he had to keep moving. "I've got some things to do," he said. "But you can walk along with me for a while."

"Still afraid of me, aren't you?" she said, falling into step alongside him. Paula had always said he was afraid of love. David believed it no more than he believed he was afraid of success—something his wife had been saying lately, to his annoyance.

David had not seen Paula since the night before Audrey had been born. They had met during a showcase of a play called *Punishment Detail*, when Paula, who was the company photographer, had taken his picture.

The showcase had been a great success. The producer had announced he was moving the play to Broadway. David's picture had appeared in the *Village Voice*, and an important agent had seen it and asked David to sign a contract.

At the closing night party, Paula had given David a look—the longest, cleanest look he had ever gotten from a woman—a look that seemed to say *I know you*. So he had taken her home and they had made love. But when he left, it was with the uncomfortable feeling that she knew him much better than he had suspected. Soon he had begun going down to her apartment two and three afternoons a week.

They had continued seeing each other even after he had told her his wife was pregnant. How he had gotten so involved with her, he couldn't understand. There were so many things he didn't like about her. She had had several actor lovers who were now famous, and she kept an envelope full of intimate letters from them on top of her bookcase. He knew this, because he had read them once, when she was out of the apartment, his face burning with shameful lust. He had the feeling she'd wanted him to do this. He hated her apartment, which she never cleaned; but he adored her sexual odor, stronger and deeper than any woman's he had ever known. This seemed dangerous to him, a sign of love. Sometimes he felt she was playing with him. When he had taken a shower and was ready to leave her apartment, she always touched him here and there, leaving her odor on him. He had to take another shower when he got home, before his wife detected it.

David was committing a great sin; he had no doubt of that. And yet, he continued to see her. He couldn't give up those long afternoons of sex, whose sheer power left him with the feeling he could walk through walls. He had never known it could be this way: like an adolescent fantasy come true. It was pure *sex*, without emotional involvements—but that, he told himself, was all it was.

That spring, *Punishment Detail* opened on Broadway, where it closed after only two performances. After he had read the terrible reviews, David told his wife he needed to be alone. Then he went down to Paula's apartment in the gray early morning light and told her that he loved her. So they had gone on seeing each other long after the show closed, into the summer, until his wife was nine months pregnant.

Finally his wife had guessed what was happening— told him when he called from a pay phone to explain for the hundredth time he'd gotten held up and would be late getting home—*David, I know.* I'm glad, he said. I'm so tired of hiding it from you. As he hung up the phone, he realized that he had made it impossible for her not to find out, knowing he was unable to stop himself, that this was the only way to end it.

The night before Audrey was born, he met Paula on a streetcorner down in the Village, and told her it was over. I've got to stop thinking of myself, he'd said. All I'm doing is hurting everyone, causing everyone pain. She reminded him that he had told her he loved her, but he ignored her pleas. My wife's having a child, he said. Maybe right now. But she had pulled him into a phone booth, leaving the door half-open so the light wouldn't go on. And they had made love standing up in the heat and smells of the city, their feet crunching on broken glass. Looking into her eyes, the eyes that seemed to know him so well, he felt the same longing he had felt atop tall buildings: to throw himself off. It would mean a long fall through divorce, disgrace, abandonment, certain death— but in the fall, there would be a moment of freedom.

Then he had practically thrown her into a taxicab and watched it drive off, promising himself he would never see her again.

They ended up at a Greek coffee shop, surrounded by more old people. David held Audrey in his lap and gave her another bottle. "I don't understand," Paula said. "You're not going to auditions anymore?"

"We're all right," he said. "My wife makes more than enough to support us."

"But you're not going to stop acting, are you?"

"No," he said. "I'll go back to it sometime. But right now, I've got more important things to do."

"I just don't want you to stop acting," she said. "You're a good actor."

"You don't understand," he said. "I've fallen in love with someone."

Paula gave him a long look.

"With Audrey," he said, looking down into her clear blue eyes. "I didn't think it would be this way, but now I wouldn't want to be away from her, not even for a day."

"I guess I can see why you'd feel that way," Paula said.

"Yes," David said. "That's how it is now."

Then he told her of the night Audrey had been born.

David and his wife had wanted a natural delivery, but her labor had been prolonged. At midnight, when she had been in labor for twelve hours, the doctor informed them he was going home. They could wait another eight hours, or he could perform a C-section. David had told his wife he loved her, and went to wait in a little room that smelled of cigarettes and dread. There he walked the floor for an hour, praying, finally, although he didn't believe, *Please God, just make everything all right.*

47

Then one of the interns came out, pulled off his mask, and glanced at David. "There's Daddy," he said. But David had still known nothing for certain until a nurse appeared and told him, "You have a baby girl." He followed her into a small room, and there was Audrey, lying on the scales, staring back at him with those blue agate eyes, a single drop of blood in her hair.

To his surprise, he felt nothing. His first thought was, *This could be anyone's baby.*

He felt nothing until the day they brought her home, in a taxicab. It was a hot, September afternoon, the air yellow with pollution, thunder rumbling in the distance. They had put her in her crib and David had stared at her for hours while she slept, until he finally fell asleep himself. She was so helpless, so delicate: It seemed intolerable she should have to exist in this hot, dirty, dangerous city. They were tearing up the street with jackhammers, and David wanted to run down and shout at them to stop making so much noise, that there was a sleeping baby up here.

It happened sometime during those first few weeks— weeks in which he got up at four o'clock in the morning to give Audrey her bottle—when they were alone in the darkness, with the hot, sooty air flowing down the air shaft, and he found himself singing softly to her. By day he learned to feed her and change her diaper. She was so tiny he could hold her with one arm, her hot little head cradled in the palm of his hand. Their apartment smelled now of a new baby, pungent but pleasant. Before long he could smell it even in his sleep. And it was not long before Audrey herself appeared in his dreams—as a terrifying responsibility, a tiny creature that he had lost somewhere in their apartment and could not find, although he could hear her crying. Then David knew he had fallen in love with his daughter.

"What I really love to do," he told Paula, "is give her a bath. The first couple of months, we used a plastic tub. But now that she's bigger, I take her in the tub with me. Babies love water," he said. "It soothes them."

Paula smiled.

"You know what she does," he said. "She tries to pick up the water. She doesn't know any better. She reaches for it and tries to pick it up, and of course it just flows right through her little fingers. And when it does, she gets this look on her face. Somehow it's the most wonderful thing," he said, "to watch her trying to pick up water."

Tears he had not expected filled his eyes.

"Yes, David," Paula said. "I can see what you mean now." She lit a cigarette. "You've fallen in love with her, all right."

The waiter brought them more coffee. Paula was looking at him in a way she had never looked at him before, and he felt he had been talking too long. He decided to change the subject. "Do you have another lover?" he asked.

"That's none of your business, is it?"

"But I want you to have another lover."

"There is someone," she said, after a while.

"That's good."

"But I don't love him as much as I loved you."

This was also good. "I'll always be fond of you, Paula," he said, putting his hand on top of hers.

"There's only one thing I don't understand," she said.

"What's that?"

"Are you and your wife sleeping together or not?"

David felt betrayed: She should not have asked this. "We're getting along a lot better than we were before," he said. "We're a lot more honest with each other. In the long run, what happened could have been the best thing for us."

"Yes, but I want to know," she said. "You told me you weren't sleeping with her before. You told me you didn't love her anymore."

Audrey pulled a fork off the table and dropped it to the floor. Suddenly she started crying, kicking. They knew so much, he thought. They sensed everything that was going on around them. His own face was burning and he felt he had to get out of there.

"I can't talk about it anymore," he said. "I've got to go."

Before she could say anything else, he got up and lifted Audrey into the Snugli. He busied himself with buttoning his jacket around her so he would not have to talk to Paula, then went to the register and paid the check. It wasn't logical, but he felt they must not talk about this in front of Audrey. She wouldn't remember the words, of course; but what if she somehow remembered the emotions? The books said every moment you spent with them was important. You had to keep holding them, touching them. Letting them know they were loved. There was no end to how careful you had to be.

They stepped outside, into the cold. The sun was sinking below the buildings. In another hour, it would be dark. Paula was just standing there, looking at him.

"I've got to be getting home," he told her.

"David," she said, "don't I mean anything to you?"

"Look," he said, "we had sex together and it was great, but that was all it was."

50

"I thought it was more than that."

"No," he said.

"Can't we see each other again?"

"That's impossible," he said. "And you know it."

"I shouldn't have asked about you and your wife. It was the wrong thing to do. This is probably the last time we'll see each other, and now this is all you'll remember."

It was as if all the light had gone out of her face.

"All right," he said. "I've got one more thing to do: stop by a friend's apartment. Why don't you come along and we can finish talking?"

"I'd like that," she said.

"But only for a few minutes."

All right, he wanted to tell her, so they'd had something like love. But there was another kind of love that had nothing to do with all this—his love for Audrey. He loved her little body, innocent of sex, loved her toes and the little cushions of fat covering the soles of her feet. He even loved her toys, the green vinyl Gumby and the bunny with glass eyes and Dynel whiskers. He loved her so much he wished she had come out of his body, and envied his wife, whose breasts, when Audrey cried, dripped tears of yellow milk. It was slightly dangerous to be alone with Paula, but he felt his love for Audrey would protect him. So they set out into the fading afternoon light, David holding his daughter before him like a shield.

The apartment was in a brownstone just off Riverside Drive. The sun was going down, and it was so cold David's fingers could hardly fit the key to the lock. They climbed four flights of stairs and walked into a studio, with two windows opening onto a tiny balcony. David spread a blanket on the floor, placed Audrey on it, and gave her a bottle.

Then he turned on the heat and watered the plants. As he did, Paula watched Audrey playing in the shaft of sunlight that fell through the windows and onto the polished wooden blocks of the floor. Two days ago, David had been here and had done the same thing. As the sun fell, the light had moved across the floor and up the wall. There, through some optical effect he could not understand, it had begun to ripple and boil, reflecting off the river somehow, turning from yellow to gold before it finally faded out altogether.

The radiator clanked, filling the room with heat. "Would you like a drink?" he asked Paula.

"Why not?"

He poured an inch of bourbon into two glasses and sat beside her on the bed.

"You're right," he admitted. "My wife and I aren't sleeping together yet."

"You weren't sleeping together before, either," she said. "That's the only thing I don't understand. Why did you decide to have a baby if you weren't sleeping together?"

He stared at his drink, wondering how he could explain.

It was true, he and his wife had conceived Audrey in a cold, conscious act, devoid of feeling—the first time they had made love in more than a year.

He struggled for words. "It doesn't have that much to do with it," he said finally.

"Yes, but it should, shouldn't it?"

It seemed to David that he and his wife had decided to have a baby because they'd stopped sleeping together. But he couldn't tell her this. It didn't make sense.

"Both of us love the baby very much," he said. "That's the important thing."

"Yes," Paula said, getting up. "I can see you're going to be a good father, David."

He was having trouble concentrating: This dry steam heat made the bourbon go straight to his head. He stood too, expecting her to move toward the door.

"There's something I'd like to do before I go," she said.

"What's that?"

"I'd like to take a picture of you giving Audrey a bath." She took a camera from her purse.

"Why do you want to do that?" he asked her.

"So I'll have something to remember you by."

He thought about the long, clean look she had given him that night, the look that had started it all.

"I guess that would be all right," he said.

David went into the bathroom, turned on the taps, and watched the tub fill with warm water. He took off Audrey's clothes; then, not looking at Paula, removed his own. Carefully he got into the tub, lowering Audrey into the water. She made sounds of pleasure. Paula stood at the door, holding the camera. He felt totally innocent. "Are you sure it's all right?" Paula asked.

"It's fine," he said.

When the flash went off, Audrey gave a gasp that turned into a laugh. Paula smiled and went into the other room. David tried to get Audrey to laugh again. His hands looked very large, closing around her little stomach. He kissed her shoulders and smelled her fine hair. "That's my girl," he said. When he lifted her from the water, her body was rosy with heat. He dried her carefully, wrapped her in the towel, and carried her into the other room.

The bathroom had been dark, and at first he couldn't see; then he made out Paula. She had taken off her clothes, and stood naked in the shaft of sunlight that seemed to ignite the floor at her feet.

David stood there for a long time, what seemed like forever, his heart pounding, before he understood the look in her eyes. *Please let me do this,* it said. *Just this once.*

He stepped forward and placed Audrey in her arms. Paula gathered Audrey to her, looking down into her clear, blue eyes; which apparently saw no difference between Paula, her mother, or any other woman. For in another moment her hand had closed around Paula's breast, and her lips had found the nipple. Then David remembered what he had told Paula, months ago, and had forgotten: *Don't you see, I wish it was you having my baby and not her?*

Paula lay on the bed, still holding Audrey in her arms. David lay beside her. Then, to his surprise, he felt himself becoming excited. He had thought this would be a moment of purity; but his body thought otherwise. He didn't want it to happen, still thought it might not happen; but then their bodies touched, and suddenly they were one, making love as effortlessly as in a dream. Paula must have wanted it, too. She was hot, lush, almost friction-less. He tried to hold back, but it was too late, he felt himself spilling, he was already there. Paula tried to hold back too, but in another moment she cried out, and a flush spread over her face and shoulders, the blood rushing into her skin. But Audrey missed it all; he was certain of that. Her eyes were held by the ripple and boil of the light on the wall above.

They lay there until the light disappeared, hearing faint traffic sounds, the singing of steam in the pipes. Then they dressed quickly, without looking at each other. The cold air downstairs was a shock.

"When can I see you again?" he asked her.

"Never," she said. "You were right, David: It's impossible."

She stooped and kissed Audrey, who was sound asleep. Then she was gone before he could say anything else, disappearing up the dark street. David watched her go, knowing that once again he had become a great sinner.

HANDS ACROSS
AMERICA

Jolene thought of it as the year the first shopping bag lady was sighted in Nortex. She had been taking the kids to school one morning in March, in a fog so thick you could see nothing but the headlights of the other cars. Suddenly a figure had loomed out of the fog, a tall woman in rags whose hair stood out in all directions, pushing a shopping cart full of her belongings right down the middle of Kemp Boulevard. Jolene had been so startled she had yelled out loud.

Several people in the neighborhood had seen her, but nobody knew who she was, or why she was forced to live this way. There was a rumor she was the wife of an oil man who had gone broke and shot himself. Nobody wanted to talk about it much. Jolene had seen shopping bag ladies on television, but she had thought this was the sort of thing that could only happen in New York City.

But then a lot of people were hurting in Nortex since the bottom had dropped out of the price of oil. Lone Star Drilling Company, one of the biggest employers in the city, had filed Chapter Eleven. Banks had already failed in Midland and Odessa, and some people were saying that the First Bank of Nortex—which had loaned Lone Star millions of dollars to build new rigs that were now turning to rust—could go belly up almost any day. Local ministers were urging a return to the traditional values of God and family. Local oil men were praying for a war in the Middle East: Another oil embargo was the only thing that could save them.

But the mayor and the city council went right on saying that if people would only vote them the funds, they could build the riverwalk that would turn Nortex into a convention center that people would flock to from all over the Sunbelt. And the paper was encouraging everyone to turn out for Hands Across America, in the hope of getting Nortex national publicity.

The kids had talked of nothing else for weeks. "But we've got to go," Jeff said when they got up that Sunday morning. "It's really important."

"I don't think they've got enough people to make it work," Jolene said.

"They might," he said, "if everybody turns out. Right around here is where they need people the most."

"If everybody in Nortex turned out, there still wouldn't be enough people to go all the way to Amarillo. Then it's got to go across New Mexico, and after that, it's got to go all the way across Arizona. There's just not enough people around here."

"But it's for a good cause," Jeff said. "It's to help starving children all over the world." He stomped into his bedroom and slammed the door.

She went to the bathroom, where Mike was shaving, and said, "Are we going to go to this thing?"

"What thing?"

"Hands Across America."

"Oh, horse shit," he said tiredly.

Mike worked for Caddo. He'd started as a roughneck, fifteen years ago. He had an office now. Lately he'd been working six days a week, but he figured he was lucky to have a job at all. Caddo was a small outfit, and hadn't overextended itself, like Lone Star.

"You'd better talk to Jeff. He's got his heart set on it. What were you going to do today?"

"Watch the Indianapolis 500, drink some beer, and take a nap."

"I sort of thought we should go too," Jolene said.

She started out putting it down, like everybody else. But when they'd started saying a couple of days ago that you no longer had to pay an entry fee, that the whole thing was going to fail unless everyone made a special effort, it sort of got to her.

"All right," Mike said. "I'll talk to him."

Jolene went into the front room, where Julie was watching *Sunday Morning.*

"Mommy," Julie said, "it's happening again. I'm picking up KNIN 1490 on my braces."

"What are they playing, honey?"

"Whitney Houston's 'The Greatest Love Ever Known.' "

She heard Mike go to Jeff's bedroom and knock on the door. When they'd lived in the apartment complex, with its Sheetrock walls, she could have heard everything they said. For a long time there was nothing but silence. Then she heard Jeff say *Oh, all right,* and heard something— probably a plastic model airplane—being thrown to the floor.

After a while the door opened and Jeff came out with a big smile on his face. "Mommy," he said, "we're going."

"He won me over," Mike explained. Then he told Jeff, "But you've got to learn to keep your temper."

Jolene put her arms around Mike. "Thanks, honey," she said.

"Oh, what the hell," he said. "I guess I'm sort of curious to see this thing for myself. And it's probably my only chance to make the *Guinness Book of World Records*."

Jolene really loved Mike. He was so good with her kids, much better than their real father. He'd bought them this house, which was the best place they'd ever lived. She couldn't understand why they wouldn't call him Dad—it really hurt his feelings—although she'd heard them do it when they were playing with other children.

They lived in one of the older parts of Nortex. Their house had been built forty years ago. It had trees in the front yard, and a porch swing, and a big backyard for the kids to play in. Both Jolene and Mike had grown up in this neighborhood. When he'd bought the house, he'd said, "Now they can have a childhood just like ours." Kids needed trees and big backyards. But the neighborhood was changing.

After lunch, Mike went out to start the car. Of course it was dead, so he had to ask Foley to get his cables and jump it. Foley was an exotic dancer. He was one of their less desirable neighbors.

"That's what you get for buying American," he was saying to Mike, when Jolene came out with the kids. Foley drove a Honda. He was right, of course. The Dodge had been worthless from the beginning. Mike had had to have the heads off after only two thousand miles.

59

"Where you going today?" Foley asked, giving Jolene the eye, like he always did.

"Hands Across America," Mike said. "What about you?"

"Oh, I'm gonna get some sleep," Foley said, smiling at Jolene. "I had a real workout last night. Some ol' lady whose husband must not have screwed her for twenty years."

At least the weather was good. Thunderstorms had been predicted, but the sky was clear. They drove out 281, passing Marley Mobile Homes, where Jolene worked. The Born Again Mobile Home Company, she called it. Her boss, Mr. Marley, belonged to the First Church of the Nazerene.

"Mommy," Julie said, "are you glad you're not at work today?"

"I sure am, honey," she said.

Mr. Marley wouldn't sell mobile homes to black people or Mexicans, because he said he always ended up having to repossess. He'd told her this after she took an application from a black airman, an officer who was going to be here for a couple of years. He also made her wear a dress to work. I don't think the good Lord minds if I wear pants to work, she'd told him, and he'd said, Suit yourself, but if you do, you'll be looking for another job.

She'd almost lost her temper. She had to watch that. She'd quit more than one job on the spot, and Mike was really counting on the money she made.

"Know who Mr. Marley told me he was going to vote for for president?" Jolene said. "Pat Robertson."

"That figures," Mike said. "Pat Robertson's the one who claims prayer can cure hemorrhoids."

They crossed the overpass by Motel 6 and turned west on Highway 90. To their surprise, there were hundreds of people standing out there in the sun. It looked like the whole town had turned out. Mike drove on, but there wasn't really any place to stop until they were halfway to Electra. Then the crowd thinned out and he found a place to pull over and park the car.

They were fifteen minutes early. The kids ran over to play on a big pile of dirt. Jolene and Mike looked around. Everyone had brought aluminum lawn chairs and thermos bottles and styrofoam coolers, and they could hear several portable radios playing. It reminded Jolene of the beach.

Mike came up behind her and put his arms around her. "Well, here we are," he said.

It was something he said when he sensed they were together. What made him say it she didn't know, but she thought he was right: They were both seeing this the same way.

They looked at the crowd. Jolene thought her children looked better than the other children, healthier. A lot of people were overweight, especially the women.

"Do you think there's something about this that appeals to people who are overweight?" she said to Mike.

"No," he said, looking at his watch. "I just think there's a lot of fat women around here."

Julie came running up and said, "I'm getting KNIN on my braces again. They're talking about Kenny Rogers. He's standing on the line between Texas and New Mexico."

"That's good, honey."

Julie ran off again.

"Can she really hear the radio on those braces?" Jolene asked.

"I think so," Mike said. "You're going to get sunburned."

He took out a tube of Coppertone and rubbed some on her nose.

61

"Hey," she said. "Have you seen that shopping bag lady lately?"

"You mean the one who pushes the grocery cart around?" Mike said. "Yeah, I have seen her. She's the worst-looking thing I've ever seen. I don't know why somebody doesn't do something about her."

"Honey, we're doing all right, aren't we?" she said.

"What do you mean?"

"I mean everything's going to be all right, isn't it?"

"Sure," he said. "Julie told me she was going to sell her braces to a museum and make lots of money."

For a while they just stood there. A couple of airplanes flew up and down the line, only a couple of hundred feet off the ground. Everyone had on bright colors, and it seemed to Jolene that people had worn their favorite clothes. She thought of the day back in high school when everyone had gotten their picture taken for the annual.

Then people began to drift toward the road. "Come on, Jeff," Mike yelled. "It's almost time."

One of the marshals stood at the edge of the highway, a fat woman whose breasts were almost pushing out of her Hands Across America T-shirt. She was waving at the cars. There were some pulling over, but a lot more were just going by.

"Come on," she said to Jolene. "Let's see if we can't get them to stop."

Jolene waved at a big black Lincoln Continental, feeling foolish. To her surprise it pulled off the road, and a man with a bushy brown beard got out.

It was Jimbo Naylor, whose family owned Lone Star Drilling Company. They hadn't seen each other since the last reunion, five years ago, but he walked right up to them and said hello. Jolene had gone out with him a couple of times in high school.

"I was going to sit this thing out," he explained. "But then I started feeling guilty. So I got in my car and started driving, and man, there's a lot of people turned out for this thing."

"There sure are."

He smiled at Jeff and Julie. "These y'all's children? Fine-looking children. I've got two myself. They're with their mother in Santa Fe. We're getting a divorce."

"I'm sorry," Jolene said.

She decided she didn't like Jimbo's beard. It might look all right in Santa Fe, but here it was definitely out of place. He looked like someone who was employed by a theme park.

Jimbo asked Mike if he was still working for Caddo, and Mike nodded. "I hope they hang in there," Jimbo said. "You know what happened to me." He held up two fingers in the Hook 'Em Horns sign. "Chapter Eleven."

She began to feel sorry he had shown up. Jimbo was rich, even if he'd lost all his money, and this was supposed to be for the little guy, to prove ordinary people could do something great.

Jimbo looked around. "I just can't get over how many people turned out for this thing."

"Yeah," Jolene said. "But there's still not enough to make it work."

"Why, that doesn't matter," Jimbo said. "The important thing is that we're here. Every person in this line is important. Y'all religious?" he asked.

Jolene felt her heart sink. "We sort of stopped going to church," she said.

"I'd lost my faith too," Jimbo said. "But not long ago, I learned a valuable lesson. Let me tell you what

63

happened to me. When my wife left me, I sort of went off the deep end. I couldn't stand that empty house, so I started going out for long drives. I found I could conduct all my business in my car—I got a cellular phone—so pretty soon I was driving all over the Panhandle, talking to bankers and lawyers and accountants. It got so I was living in my car. I don't like motels, so when I got tired, I just pulled off the road and took a nap. My car's got nice soft leather seats, and I carry a weapon, so I figured it was safe enough."

"What kind of gun you got?" Mike asked.

"Ruger Blackhawk," Jimbo said. "It's a good little weapon. But I was taking a lot of that cocaine, too, so I didn't get much sleep. Sometimes I'd drive a thousand miles before I'd call it a day. One night I was on my way to Ruidosa when I seen this big horrible object in the road in front of me. I screamed and hit the brakes. Just at that moment, I recognized it. It was the pyramid on the one dollar bill, the one that's got that big eye on top, and it was glaring right at me." Jimbo coughed into his hand and said, "There was nothing there, really. I was seeing things. But I took it as a sign I should stop pursuing the almighty dollar and find some peace in myself."

The marshal picked up a megaphone. "All right," she said. "This is it. Y'all join hands."

Jolene had been wondering all along who they would have to hold hands with.

On their left was a biker—she'd been watching him— but this one was an old guy. He wore a black Harley Davidson T-shirt and had long gray hair. His wife looked like she weighed about three hundred pounds.

On their right was a young couple. The woman's hair was dyed bright blonde. She looked to Jolene like a real whore. Her husband wore mirrored sunglasses. Their two boys wore camouflage pants and had Rambo knives strapped to their waists.

It was almost time. Silence fell.

"I'll hold your hand," the biker said to Jeff, in a surprisingly gentle voice, "if you're not afraid to hold mine."

Jimbo stood between Jolene and Mike, so she had to hold hands with him. She wondered if Mike remembered they'd dated in high school. Julie took the hand of one of the boys with the Rambo knives. Then the first song began, playing on a hundred portable radios at once, as if it was coming up out of the earth. To her surprise, Jolene did feel something, a surge of warmth going through her.

The song was serious, almost like a hymn. As each singer joined in, Julie whispered, "There's Kenny Rogers. There's Willie Nelson. There's Michael Jackson." Jolene didn't know all the words to the song. When she got to the unknown parts of the song, she just moved her lips.

When they got to the second verse, almost nobody knew the words. The singing in their part of the line stopped, and Jolene began to feel foolish again.

Mike was really getting into it. He had no idea what the words were either, but he started making up his own. "We are America," he sang,

> We stand together
> To share our bread with those
> Less fortunate than we.

Jolene was laughing a little. She couldn't help it. The woman on their right frowned at her, but Mike could be so funny sometimes.

Between the first and second songs, there was a long

wait. Everyone stared at the ground. A big truck full of cattle went by, honking its horn, and the smell of cowshit drifted over them. She felt the driver was laughing at them.

Jeff started jerking around like an idiot. "What's the matter with you?" she whispered.

"Somebody out in California stuck their finger in an electric socket," Jeff said.

The woman next to her said, "Can't you make that child behave?"

Jolene really hated people who corrected other people's children. "Why don't you mind your own business?" she said.

"Forget it, honey," the woman's husband said softly. "They're just rednecks."

She was willing to ignore that. But then Jimbo had to get into the act.

"Who you calling a redneck?" he said. "You're the one who ain't got any manners. Tell your wife to mind her own kids. These kids ain't any business of yours."

"Come on," Jolene said. "We shouldn't be fighting here."

But the woman's husband was just spoiling for it. You could tell he thought he was really hot shit. "You rednecks have got to spoil everything, don't you?" he said.

"My buddy and I went through the Vietnam thing together," Jimbo said. "You want some trouble, let's step over there. I'll give you trouble."

"Nobody wants any trouble, Jimbo," Mike said, putting his hand on his shoulder.

Just then the next song began, "America the Beautiful." Everyone stared straight ahead and started singing again. Then they got to the second verse, and once again nobody knew the words and the sound of singing died out.

But Mike kept right on singing, a big smile on his face. He knew all the words, even the part about pilgrim's feet beating a thoroughfare across the wilderness. The biker was laughing. Mike sang louder and louder, looking right at the girl's husband, until the husband looked away. Mike sounded good. He had a pretty good voice. Then the song was over, and everyone dropped everyone else's hand.

"You're all assholes," the woman's husband said. He and his wife and kids walked away.

Everyone was walking toward their cars. When she'd felt the warmth, Jolene had thought it was a big success, but now all everyone seemed to be thinking about was getting home as fast as they could.

Jimbo said, "Well, it was good to see you both. You know, I may be going back into business soon. This time, I'm only going to hire people I went to high school with. They're the only ones you can trust." He looked around, as if someone might be listening he didn't want to hear. "Something like this makes you believe in your country again," he went on. "I don't care what they say, she's great." He punched Mike on the arm. "You and I would have fought for her."

Mike smiled at him.

"If y'all would like to come out to the house," Jimbo said, "I'm not doing anything. I just built that house, you know. Now there's nobody there but me and the dogs."

"Thanks, Jimbo," Mike said. "But we've got to get the kids home."

"Some other time, then," Jimbo said, and drove off in his Lincoln Continental.

"Ol' Jimbo's going through some hard times, isn't he?" she said.

"He's done for," Mike said.

On a radio somewhere she heard an announcer saying, *Here, outside of Amarillo, Texas, a crowd of thousands gathered to see Kenny Rogers plant one foot in Texas and one foot in New Mexico. All up and down the highway, as far as the eye could see, there were people.*

They took a farm-to-market road, around the other side of Skyline Country Club, and managed to miss most of the traffic, although for some reason a highway patrol car followed them most of the way.

"Were you in Vietnam?" Jeff asked Mike, while they were stopped at a light.

"Nope," Mike said. "I sat that one out back here in the States."

"But he said you go back to the Vietnam years."

"We were in the National Guard together."

"Is that like the army?"

"Sort of, except you didn't have to go to Vietnam," Mike said. "That was why we joined," he added.

"I didn't know you and Jimbo were in the Guard," Jolene said.

"Oh, yeah," he said, laughing. "I never told you about that? Well, one week the commander decided we were getting soft, so he sent us over to this little state park near Sherman, where we were supposed to conduct patrols and pretend we were in Vietnam. It was real hot, and the first night we got eaten up by mosquitoes and chiggers. The next day, everybody was tired and hungry and bored out of their minds. Jimbo was leading the patrol. We came to this fence at the edge of the park, and on the other side we could see these naked women playing volleyball. It was a nudist camp, right next to the park.

We observed them for a while, then Jimbo proposed a search-and-destroy mission. So we swept down on them, firing blanks and throwing smoke grenades. The commander found out and we almost got court-martialed. They settled for kicking us out. So I guess I can thank Jimbo for not having to go to Vietnam." He thought for a moment, then smiled. "It was the best day I ever spent in the army."

They got home, the kids went out to play, and Jolene and Mike made love.

She fell asleep for a moment, and when she woke up, he wasn't in the bed. She walked into the front room and found him sitting, naked, on the couch.

"House is a lot bigger when they're gone, isn't it?" he said.

"What are you thinking about?" she said.

"I'm wondering if we should take out a second mortgage."

When they'd met, Jolene had been living in the big complex out by the lake. Bikers lived there, airmen, even some black people. Strangers were always coming and going, just like it was a motel. One of the bikers kept trying to hit on her. Told her she was a good-looking momma. She'd started to feel her life was going downhill, like someone in the *National Enquirer*.

Then they'd gotten married and Mike had found this house. Later they'd found out about the termites and the leaking roof, but they loved it anyway.

"I guess this neighborhood's going down," she said.

"The whole town is," he said. "But I'm glad we've got the house. It's good for the kids. They've got a big backyard here. They've got a good school. It's still a good place to grow up."

Jolene put her arms around him, thinking of the day they'd gotten married. They were going to Dallas on their honeymoon. But at the last minute, Jolene's sister had gotten sick and couldn't take the kids, so Mike had said, Hell, let's just bring 'em along. She had really loved him for that.

They'd gone to Wet N' Wild, and had a good time, even though Jeff had gotten a bloody nose on the big slide. Later they'd gone back to their motel and put the kids to bed. Then she and Mike had sat out by the pool, cars going by on the expressway, just the other side of a chain link fence, and had drunk almost a whole bottle of Jack Daniel's and promised they'd be together forever. Two days later, they had both been back at work.

The kids came back and Jolene made hot dogs, which they ate on paper plates, sitting in front of the television. On the national news, they showed pictures of the line from airplanes, taken all over the country. Then the announcer said, *Here, near the town of Nortex, in the Texas Panhandle, people turned out by the thousands, in an effort to make it all work.*

"There's our car," Julie said. "I can see our car."

"Well, I'll be goddamned," Mike said, "if that didn't look like right out there where we were."

Jolene didn't think she'd seen their car, but she thought of the way everyone had worn their best clothes, as if they were having their picture taken for the annual. That's why we did it, she thought. To get our picture taken. To prove to everyone that we were here.

She felt so good she went to the 7-Eleven for Cokes. It was something she liked to do, every so often, so she could get away from everyone and think. It was the first time in her memory that Nortex had been mentioned on the national news, and she thought that meant this had been some kind of important year. She stopped for the light at Kemp, and when she did the shopping bag lady crossed the street right in front of her, not looking left or right, pushing her cart along in a hurry as if she had someone to meet, someplace to go.

KOZMIC BLUES

In the summer of 1967 I went to San Francisco, where I lived in a walk-in closet, six feet by four, on the second floor of a big gray house on Turk Street. Six blocks away was the Haight. Two blocks downhill was Fillmore Street, the heart of the black ghetto.

For a year, ever since graduating from college, I had been suffering from a strange depression. I was living alone in Austin, wondering what to do with myself. I knew if I found a woman I would feel better, but I couldn't find one who understood me. Somehow I had to get it together—but I couldn't get it together until I found the right woman, and I couldn't find the right woman until I got it together.

My friends Larry and Cathy, who had gone out to San Francisco six months before, wrote and told me it was great. So one morning I threw my sleeping bag in the trunk of my old Chevrolet and drove out of Austin, hoping

72

that in San Francisco I could find a woman who understood me. They said it was going to be the Summer of
Love.

The trip there took three days. The desert was hot,
but it was cold and foggy the night I drove across the Bay
Bridge into San Francisco. I found Turk Street and followed it until I came to the big gray house. I had known
from their letters that they were hippies now, but it was
still a shock when Larry opened the door, wearing an Air
Force parka and love beads, his hair as long as Prince
Valiant's. Cathy stood behind him, holding a cat. We sat
on the floor, around a lamp that burned scented oil. The
walls were covered with posters for Big Brother, The Sir
Douglas Quintet, Country Joe and the Fish. I couldn't take
my eyes off their faces: They were smooth and shining
and seemed to have no muscles in them at all. "We've
gone through a lot of changes," Larry told me, his eyes
black as buttons, all pupil.

I asked them if they weren't afraid of getting busted—in
Austin, you couldn't have gone around looking the way
they did without attracting the attention of the cops.

"We've lost all our paranoia," Larry said. "And once
you lose your paranoia, it's impossible to get busted." He
told me how, when they'd first gotten here, they'd been
afraid they were taking too many drugs, burning out their
brains or something. "Then one day," he said, "we went
up on Mount Tam and took this tremendous dose of acid.
That's when we saw the Clear White Light."

"What's that?"

"Leary describes it in *The Tibetan Book of the Dead*.
You lose your ego, and then these waves of white lights
start going through you."

"The acid out here is very pure," Cathy said.

"After that, we just stopped worrying and started

73

dropping acid every day. We've probably taken it a hundred times by now."

"Everybody in this house is into acid," Cathy said. "Even the cats." She stroked the cat sitting on her lap. "Zero here's taken more than anybody. We gave him two thousand mikes."

"You've got to try some of this acid," Larry said. "We're going to open up your third eye and get you spiritual."

I didn't tell them I'd stopped taking drugs. I couldn't even smoke grass—it gave me the horrors, spells of paranoia so strong I couldn't move.

"I don't know how long I can stay," I said. "I haven't got much money."

"Don't worry about that," he said. "Pretty soon, money's going to be no problem."

I thought he meant money was going to be no problem because love would soon replace it. But it turned out he meant that he and his partner Angel were cooking up a batch of good mescaline. It was a solid deal, and I could get in on it if I wanted.

The next morning Angel showed up, a dude from Galveston who claimed to have a degree in chemistry. With him was his wife, Nova, eight months pregnant. We got in my car and followed them across the Golden Gate to Fairfax, where we parked in front of a little white frame house just off the freeway. I thought I could feel the neighbors staring at us as we got out of our cars. The kitchen was full of jars of chemicals and laboratory glassware, all of which could be seen through the window in the back door. In the bathtub, a hundred pounds of peyote buttons were cooking down to a green soup that smelled like dirty socks.

I mentioned the window and Angel said, "Yeah I caught the landlady snooping around here the other day."

"What did you do?" Larry said.

"Told her to get fucked."

Angel lit a joint and they talked about the underground economy. Angel had read an article about a hippie who had walked into a showroom and bought a Rolls-Royce right off the floor, with cash. Larry said our parents wouldn't understand, but there was really nothing wrong with what we were doing. People wanted to get spiritual, and we could help them do it. And it was going to be righteous mescaline, with no meth in it.

My paranoia was coming in waves. I lifted a blind and looked out the window. Parked down the block was a Pacific Bell panel truck, the favorite vehicle of narcs on stake-out. I pointed this out to Larry.

"Yeah," he said. "It was there yesterday, too."

Angel asked me what was wrong.

"He's got bad vibes," Larry said.

Angel shrugged and passed me the joint, the remedy for all paranoia. I could see I was making everyone uptight, so I told them I was going back to the city.

It was dark when I got back to the house on Turk Street. The moment I walked into the apartment, the telephone rang.

Larry had once been a disc jockey on the campus radio station. Now he spoke in a clear, factual voice, as if he was giving the news. "We got busted," he said. "Right after you left. This is my phone call. I want you to clean out the apartment. Do you understand?" I told him I did. He told me to come to the Marin County Courthouse tomorrow morning and hung up.

This was a role I had never played before, but I found myself performing it effortlessly. I gave the apartment a thorough search. In the closet I found a brick of grass and a baggie full of acid tabs. I dropped them in a shopping bag and went down to my car. Then I drove to the bus station, put it in a locker, and pocketed the key. It was still early, so I walked around North Beach for a while. I went to the City Lights Bookstore and bought a couple of books, then went to an all-nite cafeteria and ate chow mein. Later I drove to the beach below the Golden Gate and took my sleeping bag out of the trunk. The foghorns were blowing and a lighthouse beam flashed overhead. I scooped a hollow out of the sand for my hips, got in my bag, and lay there for the rest of the night, listening to the waves roll in.

I was no longer depressed. In fact, I felt better than I had for months. In Austin, I had sometimes spent days sitting in my apartment, wondering what to do with myself. But once I found some action to take, some role to play, I forgot myself and my depression. If only there could be a bust every night, everything would be fine.

When the sun came up, I drove back across the Golden Gate to the Marin County Courthouse, where I was told the arraignment would be at eleven. The courtroom was modern, with fluorescent lights, wooden paneling, and seats like a movie theater. At eleven, the bailiff led them in. Like me, everyone seemed to be in good spirits, even the judge. Angel had retained a hot dope lawyer named Stavros with a Zorba the Greek mustache. "Your Honor," he argued, "the federal karma in this case is just impossible." The judge released them on bond.

As we left the courthouse, Larry brought a paper from a vending machine. "Half Million Dollar Mescaline Refinery Raided in Fairfax," the headline said. "Biggest Bust In Bay Area History."

"Look at this," he said proudly. "We've hit the big time."

*   *   *

At first I liked the house, with its big bay windows and corner turrets. It was just the sort of place I had imagined myself living in. There was a big oak tree in the side yard, and a birdbath with a reflecting globe of green glass. All sorts of people lived there. Most were hippies, but there were also the retired couple who collected seashells and the two merchant seamen who lived in the basement.

When we came back from the courthouse, Larry decided it was time to get off drugs and get healthy again. This resolution lasted exactly one day, until he brought the grass back from the bus station. It was impossible for Larry not to smoke with grass in the apartment. So Cathy suggested they compromise by going on a macrobiotic diet.

The macrobiotic diet was based on the Taoist principles of yang and yin, the great polarities of the universe. Yin was the female principle, the principle of darkness, brown rice, the Beatles. Yang was the male principle, the principle of light, red meat, the Rolling Stones.

The aim was to get as yin as possible, so all we ate was brown rice, rice cakes, and a few vegetables. Most Americans were yang from eating too much sugar and red meat. This was the basic cause of the Vietnam War.

Cathy made an altar in the kitchen with a little gold Buddha she'd bought on Haight Street. We ate with chopsticks, from a common bowl. Every bite had to be chewed fifty times, to get the full food energy from each grain of rice. If you didn't, there was some danger of starving to death. Cathy closed her eyes as she ate, to maintain her concentration. Often, something I said made her lose count. By the end of the third night, all conversation at dinner had ceased. As far as I was concerned, this diet had only one advantage: It cost almost nothing.

77

After dinner, Cathy meditated in the Lotus position, wearing her headband set with chrysacola, recommended by Edgar Cayce to increase your psychic powers. Larry smoked grass and watched television. Grass and acid were all right because they were yin. Speed, alcohol, and tobacco were yang. Larry had almost stopped taking acid. One night a week, he took a light dose to watch his favorite program, *Star Trek*.

Now that I didn't smoke grass, television bored me. But Larry was inspired to deliver long monologues. The bust had made him more political. He saw signs everywhere of the coming revolution. The whole system was going to collapse—hopefully before their case came to trial. Someday soon we were going to get guns and join our black brothers in the streets. He went on and on, sounding like William Shatner, the actor who played Captain Kirk, whom he slightly resembled.

Around eleven, they went to bed. I read until the lamp ran out of oil, then tried to sleep on the floor. Zero the cat woke me by walking on my face. I was allergic to cats, and soon had a terrible cold. Sometimes I woke and heard Larry and Cathy making love.

My depression returned. A few days later, I moved into the closet.

The closet was right across the hall from their apartment. I put a pallet on the floor and unrolled my sleeping bag on top of it. There was just enough room for me, my books, and my old Smith-Corona typewriter. A light bulb hung from the ceiling. There was even a window, but it was painted over.

In the mornings, I had a bowl of rice with Larry and Cathy, then set out to explore the city. Gas was expensive, so I went on foot. For a week I walked from one end of the city to the other, looking for the same thing I had looked for in Austin—a girl.

I had hoped to get together with Sandy, an innocent young drama major I had known in Austin. When I asked Larry what she was doing, he told me she was living with a Hell's Angel and making fuck movies for the Sexual Freedom League. Sometimes I tried to talk to girls I met on the street, but my hair wasn't long enough, and they took me for an undercover cop.

There was a girl living right there in the house that should have been perfect. Her name was Dolores, and she lived alone in the turret room on the third floor. She had been out here for a year now. Dolores was an artist who worked for the Rip Off Press. She wore velvet dresses, cowboy boots, and rolled her own tortillas.

One night we all went to the Matrix to see Janis Joplin and Big Brother and The Holding Company. I'd met Janis once, when I was a freshman; and later, Larry and Cathy and I had seen her sing at Threadgill's, an Austin club. But she'd been singing folk songs then; now she was singing the blues, and she had somehow transformed herself into the greatest singer I had ever heard. She did a song that had been playing on the radio ever since I'd gotten to San Francisco:

A man and a woman need each other now, baby
To find their way in this world
I need you, baby, like a fish needs the sea
Don't take your sweet, sweet love from me.

This, I thought, was the love I was looking for: not Flower Power Love, or Hobbit Love, but the love of a real woman who had to go on loving or die.

When we got back to the house on Turk Street,

Dolores was too excited to sleep, and asked me up for a cup of ginseng tea. While she boiled water, I looked around her room. Everything was very carefully arranged: the shells and fans of coral atop the dresser, her drawing board with its pens and bottles of ink. Prisms hung on threads in the windows, turning slowly. On a bedside table I noticed *The Love Book*, by Lenore Kandel.

We sat at a table, drinking ginseng tea. I was sure we were going to make love, so sure I told Dolores everything about myself, confessed the Haight had disappointed me, even told her about my depression, and how hard it was for me to decide what to do with myself. Something about the way she listened made me think she understood.

But Dolores told me I was wrong, that the Haight was a beautiful place, we were going to generate enough love energy here to change the world. And as for my depression, all I had to do was be myself, do my own thing. The harder I tried to explain, the more depressed I got. "I've got to make a move of some kind," I said finally, not sure if I was talking about my whole life or what was going on right now, in this room.

"Then make a move," she said, smiling.

"I can't," I said, staring at the candle, which for some reason had begun to flicker very fast, like a strobe light.

"Why don't you just consult the *I Ching*?" she said. "That's what I always do."

All right, I thought. Let the *I Ching* decide. More than anything else I wanted to reach out and touch her long, flowing hair, and I told myself if I got the right answer, I would do just that.

She had the real coins, the yarrow stalks. As I threw the coins, she leaned forward.

I got the Po hexagram: Falling Apart. The commentary said, "It will not be advantageous to make a move in any direction whatsoever."

The summer wore on. Fog hid the sun for days at a time. Larry watched television. Cathy made god's-eyes, crosses of sticks woven with colored yarn. It was a job that would have bored a child of nine, but one she performed by the hour. In June, Cathy decided we weren't getting spiritual enough, so we went on Diet Number Seven—brown rice alone.

I had no energy at all. My lips were always numb, my clothes no longer fit. Larry said it would be good for me: the Vietcong lived on only one bowl of rice a day. Cathy promised me that if we followed this diet, we would lose our egos completely and be able to trip without taking drugs.

Down on Fillmore Street, next to Do City, where the brothers got their hair conked, was a joint called The Pig Stand. Every day I slipped down there and bought a hot pork sausage for fifty cents. The floor was tacky with grease and there was a photo of Huey Newton on the wall. The brothers hanging around outside sometimes called me a hippie motherfucker, but hunger drove me to ignore the bad vibes.

The spades, as they were called then, were getting angrier every day. There were riots in Harlem and Oakland. Detroit was in flames. There was a strange expectancy in the air. This city's going to burn, people said gleefully. It's going to burn right to the ground.

Larry's case, on the other hand, was going well. Stavros had gotten the charges against Cathy and Nova dropped, and it looked as if he and Angel might get only three years probation for the manufacturing of mescaline. Larry decided to give a party for the whole house to celebrate.

I spent that day as I spent every day—at the Strand Theatre, down in the Tenderloin, where I paid a quarter for a ticket and sat among the winos for four hours, watching a double feature of *The Big Country* and *Flying Leathernecks*. Then I went to the Haight, where I walked the streets under a sky the color of ice.

It seemed to me that things were taking a change for the worse. There were still a few lovely hippie girls, but most of them looked like they were burned out on drugs. Everywhere I went, someone either asked me for spare change or tried to sell me crystal meth.

My depression never left me now. I seemed to weigh thousands of tons. I was the heaviest guy in the whole Haight-Ashbury—the only guy who wouldn't smoke grass or take acid, the only guy who hadn't found peace, love, and spiritual bliss. I would have gone back to Austin, but a few days before my car had broken down. Anyway, something told me there was no going back. Now that my depression had reached this level, it would be waiting for me wherever I went. Time seemed to have stopped, and I had the feeling nothing would ever happen to me again. This, I thought, was my punishment for not letting myself get drafted and sent to Vietnam.

When darkness fell, I walked back up Fillmore. Just before I got to The Pig Stand, I noticed a crowd of spades on the sidewalk ahead, some shouting, some laughing. A burglar alarm was ringing insistently.

Suddenly a Molotov Cocktail hurtled through the fog and exploded on the roof of a parked car. The spades cheered as if it were a football game. I had never seen a car burn before, and stood watching until someone threw a bottle at me, then I ran for my life.

Two blocks up Turk Street, I stopped and looked downhill. The riot was definitely on. As I watched, the cops arrived and blocked off the intersection. There was a building on fire further down. It sent up a hovering cloud of orange smoke, shot through with little comets of burning tar.

Upstairs, the party was going strong. Everyone was there—the couple who danced for the San Francisco ballet, the girl who made jewelry out of chicken bones, even the two merchant seamen, who were drinking wine and giving everyone surly looks. Dolores was standing at the window. She wondered what would happen if the spades broke into the house. Frank, a political science major at Berkeley, told her there was nothing to worry about. "They don't really hate white people," he said. "All they're after is material goods. If they come here, we'll just throw open our doors and tell them to take our television sets." Just then a gang of kids came running up Turk Street, throwing bottles. "Shit," Larry said. "I wish I'd bought that gun. I'd be out there too."

Everyone was having a great time. It was just like the bust—everyone had feared it, but when it really happened, it wasn't the worst thing after all. Someone passed a joint, and someone else put on "Light My Fire."

But I was depressed, for nothing had really happened: The city hadn't burned down, and tomorrow would be just like today. So I took to the closet, where I stared at the light bulb and thought of the only thing that was real to me anymore, the past—in particular, the night, five years ago, when I had met Janis Joplin.

A friend had introduced us—they both lived in Scottish Rite Dormitory, notorious for its homely girls. Janis and I had walked in the park and talked. She had been a beatnik, one of the handful of students who wore black clothes and hung out in the Student Union. I had just read

On The Road, and liked the idea of hitchhiking around the country, looking for kicks and truth.

We had talked about how much we hated our hometowns. She was from Port Arthur, and I had just spent a weekend there. I told her how I had gotten drunk and climbed around on the girders of a big suspension bridge over a ship channel, the sort of thing Dean Moriarty would have done. I told her how I had stood on a girder and looked through the fog at the shrimp boats chugging out to the Gulf, hundreds of feet below.

Later, my friend had told me Janis liked me, and I should ask her for a date. But I hadn't. Something about her had put me off. Now she was famous, a great artist, a woman thousands of men dreamed of making love to. And I was living in a closet, slowly starving to death while I read *Zap Comix* and *The Sickness Unto Death.*

I clung to the memory of that night. It was beginning to seem like the only important thing that had ever happened to me. I still thought I could get it together—if I found the right woman. But this was no ordinary depression, and no ordinary woman would do. She had to have suffered, like I was suffering. I had the Kozmic Blues, and I needed a woman like Janis to love my troubles away.

In fact, it had begun to seem to me that Janis was the only woman who could save me.

By August, I knew I was in deep trouble.

Larry and Cathy had run out of money and had gone back to the post office, where they worked, like lots of hippies, sorting mail. I spent my days alone.

After two months of fog, the days had suddenly become clear and hot. One morning I took my typewriter and climbed the fire escape to the roof, where I tried to write letters. Zero the cat joined me while I typed, sitting by the chimney, under the television antenna. The roof was covered with blue composition shingles, shaped like fish scales.

For a while I lay on the edge of the roof and looked down five stories to the sidewalk and the iron pickets of the fence. For some reason this made me feel better.

Then I grew restless and knew it was time to move. I rode the bus downtown to the Strand Theatre. I no longer bothered to look in the paper and see what was playing. Anything was all right with me. When I went to the bathroom to weigh myself, there were two sailors having sex in a toilet stall. I dropped a penny in the scale, and discovered I weighed thirty pounds less than I had in June.

I sat through *The Thief of Baghdad*, trying to lose myself in what was happening onscreen, wondering how I was going to get out of this. My mind worked at incredible speed, flashing through thousands of choices in an instant. Just when I thought I had everything worked out, it all fell apart.

When I came outside, I caught sight of my reflection in a store window. I finally looked like a hippie now. I had also worn the same clothes for a week, even when I slept. I caught a bus across town to the Haight.

I walked the streets with the Kozmic Blues, past the Hobbit Hole and the Love Burger, to Tracy's Doughnut Shop. It was sometimes called the Crystal Cafe because a lot of meth-heads hung out there, and it was a very bad place. I sat at the counter and ordered a cup of coffee.

There was a girl sitting next to me who wore an Afghani coat of yellow hide, lined with goatskin. She had a red diamond painted on her forehead, and she was blowing bubbles. After a while, the guy behind the counter told her to stop or get out.

I bought her a cup of coffee and a doughnut and she gave me a big acid grin. Her name was Wendy. She was a triple Pisces, and she had run away from her parents in Los Angeles. I told her I was from Texas, and she thought that was groovy.

She said she was going to Chocolate George's funeral. Chocolate George was a Hell's Angel who'd gotten killed a couple of days before. She knew some of the Angels, and they were beautiful guys. Big Brother and the Grateful Dead were giving a memorial concert in the park after the funeral.

"I'll go with you," I said, thinking I would get to see Janis.

Outside, she asked me if I'd like to drop some out-of-sight acid, and I said sure.

"Hold out your hand," she said. She took a Pez candy dispenser from her purse, each colored wafer a tab of Orange Sunshine.

I swallowed one before I could stop myself. Just for a moment I felt fear, as I always did when I dropped acid. Now there was no going back. Ahead was some great transition in time and space. But I hadn't taken drugs all summer, and it had done nothing for me. I wanted to be like everyone else: meet a girl on the street, drop some acid, maybe get laid.

We watched the Angels come rumbling up Haight on a phalanx of motorcycles.

As we started walking toward the park, I could already feel the acid coming on, in sickening little flashes. "You talk like a cowboy," Wendy said, "so I'm going to call you Cowboy." I told her that was fine with me. She told me about the place where she was staying, a crash pad on Waller. "There's all kinds of beautiful people there," she said. "It's run by this woman who used to be a nun. You can come over there after the concert and meet everybody. You can crash there if you want."

We entered the park. More bubbles floated by. The sky was getting too bright to look at, and I could hear what sounded like electronic music. Up ahead there was a great crowd of hippies, men, women, and children. There was a flatbed with microphones on it, and a humming generator truck. There were kegs of beer on crushed ice for the Angels, who had pulled up their bikes in front of the flatbed and stood there with folded arms, staring back at the crowd through sunglasses.

"Let's get closer," she said, "so we can really experience the music." We found our way through the crowd and sat on the grass right in front of the Angels. Somebody offered me a joint and I pretended to take a hit off of it.

Just then the music started, the loudest sound I had ever heard in my life. I looked up and saw Janis towering over me. She looked enormous. I closed my eyes and listened to her sing, losing myself in the acid. I flashed through other times and places. Once I thought we were sitting together in the park back in Austin. "Down on me," she sang, "down on me."

> Looks like everybody
> In the whole wide world
> Is . . . down on me.

She seemed to be singing right to me.

And then I saw her—saw her more clearly than I had ever seen her before; saw her with the all-seeing eye of acid, like the diamond Sabu had stolen from the forehead of the great goddess in *The Thief of Baghdad*. I understood then what it was that thrilled everyone: It was the hunger in her voice.

Her amplified voice cut through me like a knife, and I heard it as a cry for help—a cry for love. She was starving for love, like I was. She needed love desperately, she was suffering from the same all-consuming hunger, a hunger that could kill.

Then the song was over, and everyone was on their feet.

"Where are you at, Cowboy?" Wendy shouted in my ear.

"Back in time and space," I said.

Janis was singing again. I looked away, and caught sight of Wendy, who had taken off her top and was dancing. She had large breasts, covered with goosebumps, that bobbed this way and that.

A blow on my head knocked me senseless. One of the Angels had thrown a snowball made of crushed ice. I picked myself up and got another one in the face.

The Angels were laughing. People started moving away from me. It wasn't good when the Angels singled you out.

One of them was standing in front of me. I gave him a sick grin.

"Peace, brother," he said.

I held up two fingers.

"I'm gonna dance with your ol' lady. You mind?" He grabbed Wendy and pulled her toward the stage. She didn't seem completely sorry.

I walked away through the crowd and on into the park. For a long time I could hear Janis singing behind me. Then she blended into the electronic music.

Soon I was lost. I stumbled through a thicket of rhododendron, whose clinging, erotic smell almost overwhelmed me. Ahead I heard the ringing of wind chimes. I came out in a garden, with a strange little wooden bridge and an iron statue of Buddha. I seemed to be in Japan.

Tourists were walking the paths. "Look," one said, "there's a hippie," and took my picture.

I splashed across a stream, onto a little island covered with moss, where I sat on a rock. My body was shuddering, and I knew I had taken an enormous dose of drugs.

Then I remembered what Janis and I had talked about that night in the park, as clearly as if she were sitting there with me. I had been telling her about climbing around on the girders of that bridge, looking down at the water far below. And when I had told her, she had smiled, and I had seen a longing in her eyes and seemed to hear a ringing noise, like the shrilling of locusts on a summer night, that had filled me with terror.

Some sort of wind blew me off the rock and into space, where I floated for an infinite time in a clear white light.

This, I thought, has gone on long enough. You have followed this as far as you want to go. This is going to be your undoing.

Yes, I thought, but how do I get out?

There's a way, said a voice.

What?

You can walk.

Could it be as simple as that?

Yes. You can walk back to Texas, if necessary. You can do it. All you have to do is take the first step.

I opened my eyes and found myself lying on the grass, my heart pounding. I got to my feet, feeling a boundless energy.

So I walked. That was what I did best. From the time I was a child, I had loved to walk. That was my destiny, to walk for years, until I was an old man, going everywhere, seeing and hearing everything along the way.

The fog rolled in again, and the sky turned a glowing pearl gray. I walked for a long time, my body still shuddering, snot pouring out of my nose, full of acid joy. At first I was alone, but as darkness fell I sensed others with me. I found myself joining a great silent crowd of people, all moving toward the entrance to the park.

Wendy was waiting by the gate. I wasn't even surprised. This happened on acid all the time: You lost people, then found them again. I had come back to where I started, but this time I wasn't going to get caught up in the circle.

"Hey, Cowboy," she said. "Where are you going?"

"Baby," I said, "I'm going home."

I phoned my parents and asked them to send me some money. The first thing I did was go to a cafeteria and eat a large meal of roast beef and mashed potatoes. When I got my car fixed, I put up a notice on the bulletin board of the Free Clinic. In another day I had three riders who wanted to go to Austin and were willing to share gas money.

Three days after what proved to be my last acid trip, Larry and Cathy told me they were going to get married. They phoned their parents, who didn't seem to think it made much difference—they'd been living together for years—but I did. They had made a decision. What had been so hard for me proved easy for them.

Larry asked me to be his best man. He even gave me a book on weddings explaining my role. One of my duties was to make arrangements with the minister, and Larry wanted the ceremony performed by the minister of the church next door.

That afternoon I went to the little red granite church. An elderly black man in a blue suit answered the door.

I explained what I was there for, and he asked me upstairs. His wife was clearing plates from the table, and his grandchildren sat on the floor in front of the television, watching cartoons. It was a black and white television, but a plastic sheet had been taped to the screen to give the illusion of color: The top of the sheet was blue for the sky, the middle pink for faces, the bottom green for the earth.

I told him that we wanted a simple ceremony, that these were two young people in love who sincerely believed in Jesus Christ. I don't know if he believed me, but he agreed to do it.

Larry and Cathy had asked everyone in the house, but for one reason or another almost nobody could come. But Angel and Nova were there with their child, Bilbo; and one of the merchant seamen surprised everyone by showing up in a coat and tie. Larry had shaved off his beard and Cathy carried some daisies she'd picked in a vacant lot off Haight. The ceremony was held in the yard. I gave Larry the ring, he placed it on Cathy's finger next to the reflecting globe of green glass and the preacher pronounced them husband and wife.

I found I enjoyed playing the role of best man. Afterwards, I gave the minister twenty-five dollars. He said they seemed to be fine young people, and I agreed. I asked him if he wouldn't like to come to the reception, but he said he had to prepare a sermon. I held open the gate for him. He nodded to me, then walked slowly down the steep hill toward the church.

Upstairs, everyone was eating cake and drinking Almaden pink chablis. Cathy had decided to depart from Diet Number Seven for one day. No honeymoon was planned: They both had to work at the post office the next day.

Dolores had been invited, but hadn't showed. I asked Cathy why. "I don't know," she said. "She had a thing going with this guy that didn't work out. She's been going through a lot of changes lately."

I had a glass of wine, then left through the kitchen window. Nobody saw me go. I took the fire escape to the roof and climbed across the hot shingles to the very top.

Zero the cat had followed me. He rubbed along my thigh, purring. For a while I stared down at the dull yellow concrete, a hundred feet below. Then I looked up. It was another hot, clear day, the clearest yet. To the west, I could make out a range of emerald mountains I had never seen before, under piled-up cumulus clouds, white as marble.

I envied Larry and Cathy. I was getting out of here, but I wanted to be like them. I wanted to get stoned, to get married by a black preacher. To be a good hippie. Most of all, I wanted to be in love.

For a while I stared at the hills, then I went down and knocked on the door of Dolores's apartment. Her face had changed; I noticed that the moment she opened the door.

"We were expecting you at the wedding," I said, feeling a little giddy from the wine. She stared at me. I was wearing a loud paisley tie I'd bought on Haight Street. It made me feel silly, as if I were in costume, but also free to do and say anything I chose.

"Well, I thought I might come, but now I don't know," she said. Her voice was toneless. She stood aside and I walked in. She didn't seem to care one way or the other.

I looked around, at the fans of coral, the shells, the blue glass jars of herbs. Her copy of the *I Ching* was open on the table.

"I don't know," she said. "I just can't seem to get it up to do much of anything. I've been throwing the Ching, but it hasn't been very good to me lately. The other day I was going to go out and buy some groceries, but the Ching told me not to, so I stayed here. Same thing with the wedding. I wanted to go. I really dig Larry and Cathy. But this morning it told me there would be Initial Difficulty, a pit, danger."

"Why don't you come down and have a glass of wine?" I said. "That'll make you feel better."

"I just hate to leave this room," she said. "Everything's getting so ugly. Have you noticed how many freaked-out people there are on the streets? There's just too many people here now. And my friends are going through some bad changes. It's getting so I'm afraid to go out, so I just sit here all day and throw the Ching. Sometimes I throw it twenty or thirty times a day."

"Nothing bad could happen to you downstairs," I said.

She sighed and sat down at the table. Then she threw the coins and I found myself holding my breath. They clicked loudly in the silence, like stones clicking together underwater.

She turned the pages of the Ching. "Well," she said, after a while, "I got the Perilous Pit. That's K'an above and below. Water, a pit, danger. There will be evil for three years."

She gave me a pale smile. "That doesn't sound too good, does it?"

"I'll be downstairs," I said, "if you decide to come."

I left her at the window, staring at the prisms turning in the sunlight.

STORMCHASER

They were coming back from Amarillo, pulling a hundred cars of coal. At Chillicothe, they stopped to let the hotshot go by, and Burl walked back up the tracks to throw the switch.

It was the first hot day of the year. His boots crunched on the cinders, and the wind stirred his hair. Burl had long blonde hair, long as a girl's. When he'd first started working for the railroad, two years ago, some of the boys had threatened to cut it off for him with a pair of rusty scissors. But then they'd forgotten about it, just like they forgot about everything else.

He leaned into the switch and watched the tracks slide into place. Then he lifted his lantern to signal the engineer. The engineer gave the air horn a blast to let him know he'd seen him. Burl rolled a cigarette, enjoying the heat. Something, the light, or the feeling of the air, or the time of day, made him look to the west. That was when he saw it, the nickel-gray dome of a big cumulonimbus, almost transparent at this distance, fifty or a hundred miles off.

He felt his heart pound. The first thunderstorm of the year. A cold front was moving down across the Panhandle. There would be storms tomorrow. He'd been waiting all winter for this. He stared at it for a long time. Then his eyes dropped, and he saw the big rattlesnake sleeping next to the rail, inches from his boot. After a moment, he smiled.

John was waiting for him by the caboose. "What took you so long?"

"Almost stepped on a big rattlesnake."

"How big?"

"Three feet long, maybe four."

John was older than Burl, about forty. He was the only guy at the railroad Burl could talk to. When John was younger, he'd dropped out of Bible college and had gone on a search—studied philosophy, history, psychology. He really knew a lot of things.

"Look over there," Burl said. "There's a big thunderhead."

John shaded his eyes with his hand. "Think there'll be tornadoes tomorrow?"

"Could be."

"What are you gonna do?"

Burl grinned. "Take a day off and go chasing 'em."

"I been thinking about taking a day off myself."

"All right," Burl said. "You can go with me."

Burl was into chasing tornadoes. He'd started doing it last spring, spending his days off watching the weather service channel, waiting for storms to develop.

At the right moment, he got in his old red Mustang and drove out into the Panhandle to meet them, his CB tuned to the local storm spotter net. When they patched into the weather service in Fort Worth, he could hear the meteorologist tell them which storm was going to produce a tornado.

The great thing was to find a storm nobody else had found, not even the vehicles from the Severe Storms Laboratory, up in Norman, Oklahoma, which had Doppler radar. Then he got as close as he could, pulled off the road, and got out, in the strange silence and strange light under the base of the storm, and watched the funnel trying to form. It was another world under there, where the clouds boiled. He always felt being there left him changed, but in what way he couldn't say.

They rolled back to Nortex, getting in late that night. Burl went home and dreamed he stood in the backyard of the house where he had grown up. The air was dense, threatening. Looking to the west, he saw funnels dropping from the clouds.

He woke at eleven o'clock and looked out the window. The sky was cloudless, the sun hot. He showered and made a pot of coffee. Then he fried himself some bacon and eggs and ate them sitting in the front room, looking out the window at the sky.

Pretty soon John drove up in his old International pickup. He'd brought a bottle of Herradura Tequila, hecho en Mexico, and a Polaroid camera. "I thought I might get some pictures," he explained.

He showed Burl the paper. There had been tornadoes in the Panhandle last night. A mobile home park had been destroyed near Snyder.

"I don't see why you got to go out and chase tornadoes," he said. "Thing you should do is just live in a mobile home. They always head straight for 'em."

"I've thought about it," Burl said.

"How does it look for today?"

Burl turned the television to the weather service channel. The air was unstable, full of moisture, and the jet stream was right overhead. A dryline was forming to the west. "Couldn't be better," he said. "We're gonna have storms popping up all over around three o'clock this afternoon. All we've got to do is find the right one."

"Think you can do that?"

"I'm gonna try."

"I sure hope so," John said. "I took a day off, you'd better find me a tornado."

That was the trouble with working for the railroad. You never knew how much time you were going to have off. When you came back from a trip, you put your name on the bottom of a list. You might have to go back to work in eight hours, or eighty. There was no way to tell.

John read Burl the rest of the paper. Most of the articles had to do with the collapse of the oil business. But everything would be all right, the editor said, if only people would have more faith in Ronald Reagan. And there was a good side to this: People were rediscovering their faith in the Lord. A record turnout was predicted for the annual Easter pageant at the Holy City, up in the Wichita Mountains.

"When I was a kid I played a part in that show," John said. "I played a little boy who brought a gift to the Baby Jesus. My father played John the Baptist." He sighed and closed the paper. "What do we do now?" he said.

"There's nothing to do but wait."

John took off his shirt and lay on a towel in the front yard. Burl plugged in his guitar and sat on the couch, where he could watch television as he played.

Things, as John said, had sure gone to shit here in North Texas. He hated working for the railroad, but he knew if he quit he could never find another job. And now his father had cancer—he'd gotten it at the same time the bottom had dropped out of the price of oil.

If he hadn't flunked out of college, or if the group he'd played for hadn't broken up, things might have been different. But there was no sense in thinking about it.

Sometimes he had the feeling the whole world was falling apart. He'd started seeing a lot more Mexicans on the train, too, even all the way up here. You used to see maybe one or two a year, but last month he'd dropped down into a gondola and had found eight or nine all huddled together, looking at him with those sleepy Indian eyes. You were supposed to turn them in, but he'd gone back to the caboose and brought them his lunch, and told them, in his stumbling high school Spanish, how to get off before they got to the Amarillo yards.

He got up and went to the icebox for a beer. John came in and said, "Why'd you stop playing?"

"I lost my inspiration."

"Maybe you need some of this," John said, offering the bottle of Herradura.

"I don't need to get drunk," Burl said.

"No," John said. "What you need is a girl. If you had a girl, you wouldn't be out following tornadoes around."

That was the truth. But he couldn't seem to get one. It was hard, when you never knew if you were going to be in town more than another eight hours.

They watched television, switching from the weather service channel to the soaps to Country Music Television. There had to be storms today. If there weren't, he would have wasted his first day off in months.

By two o'clock, he thought he couldn't stand it any longer. They watched a Marie Osmond video he'd already seen a thousand times. It started with her giving a concert everybody loved. When she was finished she left, stopping only to give an autograph to a little girl. She got in a limousine and gave a big sigh to show you she was sick of the whole thing. Then she got into a Learjet, which took off into the fog. It cut to her getting out of a helicopter the next morning, somewhere up in the mountains. She got in a Bronco, happy now, and drove over a stream and up to a log cabin that must have cost a million dollars, where a little boy was waiting for her.

"She likes the simple life, don't she?" John said.

"She's full of shit," Burl said. Every time he saw that video, he felt the same dull anger.

He switched to the weather service channel and saw the first faint blue echo of a storm north of Seymour.

"Here we go," he said, suddenly alert. "Now we're going to get some action."

The echo went from blue to green as the tops built above twenty thousand feet. The meteorologist called from Fort Worth and told the spotters to get ready to go out.

Standing on the back porch he could see the anvil top of the storm spreading out to the west, glaring white in the sun, big as the cloud from a hydrogen bomb.

John was asleep on the couch. "Come on," Burl said, shaking him: "Let's go for it."

They got in the Mustang and headed out of town on 287. John hung his head out the window, his eyes closed and his mouth open, drinking in the air. Burl had to smile: He looked just like a dog.

The storm was headed to the northeast, toward Oklahoma. It was big, a good forty miles long, the anvil blowing out another fifty miles ahead of it on the jet stream. Under the core, where it was raining, it looked black as night. He could hear the storm spotters talking on the CB.

I'm sitting at Maybelle Corner, one said. *Man, it's sure getting dark over there to the west.*

Burl had learned to look for that blackness. The most intense storms seemed to radiate some kind of *black energy.* He was sure there was a tornado in that storm.

At Electra, he turned off on a little blacktop road going southwest, through open range country, that would take them under the core.

It was like driving right up to the edge of the world. Behind them they could see a little daylight, and the hill called Medicine Mound, where John had told him the Comanches used to eat peyote and have visions. But up ahead everything stopped at a wall of rain, sharp as a knife and black as outer space.

Burl pulled off the road a mile short of it and they got out. The storm was passing right in front of them. The air was dead still. A pumping jack nodded in the mesquite a mile away, its chugging diesel the only sound.

"I'm scared already," John said.

The silence was what got to you. It was like watching a hundred-car train roll by and hearing nothing.

"If there's a tornado, it's on the other side of that rain," Burl said. "There's nothing to worry about here, except lightning."

John looked at him.

"I'm not joking," he said. "More people have been killed by lightning than tornadoes."

"I didn't think of it as a joke," John said. "Is there any way to tell where it's going to strike?"

"The highest thing around, or the biggest concentration of metal," he said. "Like that pumping jack." *Or this car,* he thought.

Burl stared at the storm through his binoculars. Sometimes, when people asked him why he chased tornadoes and he wanted to annoy them, he told them he was looking for God.

In one of his meteorology books there was an account by a man who had looked up into the mouth of a funnel when it had torn off the roof of his house. Suddenly, he had been able to hear nothing except for the beating of his heart. He had looked up and had seen the interior of the funnel was composed of rings, hundreds of rings that looked hard as steel, going all the way to the top, where a strange blue light shone down. Then the ring at the top had moved, and the next one had slid over to get underneath it, and in this way a sort of ripple had run all the way down until it reached the mouth of the funnel, which had jumped over him and moved on.

Seeing those rings would be better than seeing God. Just thinking about them made his heart pound.

A couple of drops of rain fell. An instant later, a bolt of lightning hit the pumping jack.

Burl screamed and threw himself to the ground. At the blue-violet moment of the flash, he thought it had hit the car. The thunder was deafening, like tons of falling stone.

John was looking down at him with a smile. "Get in the car," Burl yelled, picking himself up.

"You were scared," John said, as he fumbled for the keys. "You were scared shitless."

"That was nothing," he said. "Wait until one hits close enough so you can hear the plasma snap. Sounds just like grease on a hot stove."

The meteorologist was talking to the spotters. *That storm has split into two cores*, he said. *We've got a hook echo in the one to the north. That's the cell we want you to concentrate on.*

Burl let out a yell. "You hear that?" he said. "A hook

echo—that means a tornado." He started the car and pulled out onto the road.

"What should I do?" John said.

"Get that camera ready. If we start hitting hail, that means we're getting close to the funnel."

Just before they hit the rain, they passed one of the spotters, sitting by the side of the road in a Toyota pickup. Burl stepped on the gas and shot him the finger. A moment later, they heard him say, *There goes that goddamned red Mustang again.*

Then they were in the rain, so heavy he had to turn on the headlights to see the road. The Mustang, being a Ford, was worthless except for the purpose of chasing tornadoes. It was fast, and it was so old the rubber had completely worn off the top, leaving a lid of rusted metal. In another moment hailstones as big as golfballs were bouncing off of it. John took a big gulp of Herradura. Burl was laughing insanely, like he always did. He knew they could be driving right into the mouth of the funnel. Then he saw light up ahead, and a moment later they were breaking out, into the world he loved.

The base of the storm pressed right down on their heads. It was like being in a room twenty miles long and only a few hundred feet high. To the southwest a little daylight seeped in under the edge of the storm, but it was the dim orange of light from a sodium vapor lamp. All he could see was black mesquite and the wet road, like a ribbon of mercury reflecting that horrible orange light. He looked around in the almost total darkness, but there was no funnel to be seen. Just to the north, he made out a boiling confusion of clouds that looked like they were right down on the ground.

He took another blacktop going in that direction, and a moment later they passed snapped-off trees, a herd of frightened cattle, and an old Aeromotor windmill blown to the ground.

"It's right up ahead of us," he shouted to John. But now they had to catch it, and the storm was moving fast. They passed the power plant at Oklaunion and crossed the Red River on a little concrete bridge. On the other side, the pavement stopped. They were in Oklahoma now, and there was nothing between here and Lawton but dirt roads, small farms, and abandoned Atlas missile silos. "Find me a good road going north," he yelled at John, throwing him the map.

The storm was moving out in front of them. A great shaft of sunlight poured down, and when it did he saw more hailstones scattered everywhere, white as eggs in the sun.

"Storm's heating up again," he said. "Get that camera ready."

They met a biker on a big Harley chopper, and Burl wondered what he was doing out here in the middle of nowhere. Then they topped a little rise and saw a figure walking toward them.

When they got a little closer they could see it was a woman, walking right down the middle of the red clay road.

She had long black hair, parted in the middle and plastered down by the rain, and wore a dirty white leather jacket that looked like she'd bought it at a thrift shop.

Burl slowed down so he wouldn't splash her, then drove right past her. "Ain't you even going to stop?" she yelled, and he hit the brakes.

John said, "We can't leave a woman in distress."

"We've got to catch that storm."

John looked over his shoulder. "She's a pretty good-looking woman."

Burl looked in the mirror. She had picked up a hailstone and was about to fling it. "Hey," he yelled, "you don't have to do that." He put the Mustang in reverse and backed up.

"What's the trouble?" he said.

"My ol' man kicked me off his scoot," she said. "Think you could give me a ride to Lawton?"

"We're not going that way."

"Well, then, give me a ride to a telephone. You can't leave me here." She had a big red bump on her forehead, and her clothes were soaked.

"All right," Burl said. "Get in."

She climbed in the backseat and he stepped on the gas. The storm was getting ahead of them, but if he found a good road he could still catch it. "You have a fight with your ol' man?" John asked her, handing her the bottle of Herradura.

"We were going to Crowell to see his mother," she said. "Then we started fighting, and he told me to get my butt off and drove away. Then it started to hailing."

"Pretty inconsiderate," John said.

She took a big pull from the bottle. "I thought I was going to get stoned to death, like some woman in the Bible."

They jolted along the muddy road. She told John she was a Cherokee. Her ol' man was a half-blood. He belonged to the Renegades, a motorcycle gang Burl had heard a lot about. They were supposed to be really bad dudes.

She leaned over the seat, breathing in his ear. "You got the prettiest long hair," she said. "You look just like David Lee Roth."

"Burl used to be a rock and roll star," John said. "Played guitar for 'Uncontrolled Meltdown.' "

"You're shitting me," she said. "That was a really great group. Whatever happened to you guys?"

"We broke up," Burl said, turning onto another muddy road just like the first. Forty was as fast as he could go. "Just stay on that goddamned map," he told John.

"What's your hurry?" she said.

"We're chasing a tornado," Burl said.

She looked at John, then back at Burl. "Let me get this straight," she said. "You're chasing a tornado? What in the hell for?"

"This is a spiritual quest," John said. "You're an Indian girl. Ain't you never read Carlos Casteneda? We're looking for power, big medicine. Hoping to see Mescalito."

She took another pull from the bottle. "You're a couple of insane mothers, aren't you?" she said.

They came to a blacktop going north. Burl stepped on the gas, and for three or four miles he was doing eighty. Then he saw a line of cottonwoods up ahead where there was a small town. He slowed down to go through the single traffic light.

"There's a 7-Eleven," she said. "They probably got a telephone."

"And I could use something to eat," John said. "Just a couple of sticks of beef jerky to keep me going."

"We're not stopping."

"Well, you're almost out of gas," John said, pointing to the gauge. "You're not gonna be chasing any tornadoes on a dry tank."

Burl pulled in, disgusted with himself for not getting gas before they left. John and the girl went inside, and he filled the tank as fast as he could, looking at the blackness

105

to the north. A couple of bolts of lightning stabbed down. He was close enough so he could hear the thunder.

When he went inside to pay, John was buying a couple of six-packs of beer, sticks of jerky, and beer nuts from the fat woman behind the register.

Burl asked him where the girl was.

"In the can," John said.

He pounded on the door. After a while he heard the toilet flush and she came out. "You ain't got very good manners, do you?" she said.

"Just make your phone call," he said.

John was talking to the fat woman, who was watching her little Sony television, telling her about a big catfish he'd caught on bloodballs. "Excuse me," the girl said. "Could you give me some change for the pay phone?"

"It's out of order," the woman said.

In the parking lot, she turned to Burl. "Which way are you going now?"

"Whichever way that storm goes."

"It's going toward Lawton," she said. "So I guess I'll stay with you for a while."

"Fine," John said, before Burl could protest. "Let's get in the car and I'll open us a beer."

Then they were back on the road and doing eighty again, Burl hoping they could still catch the storm. John looked at the map. "We're coming to Chattanooga pretty soon," he announced. "I know that town." John had been everywhere. "There's a little café in that town that's got the best catfish in Oklahoma."

"We're not stopping," Burl said.

"I'm just pointing out some of the more interesting things about this part of Oklahoma."

"I love catfish," the girl said.

"So do I," John said. "In fact, one time, when I was going to helicopter school, down at Mineral Wells, me and a buddy of mine borrowed a chopper and hopped over here for some catfish. Put her down in a field somewhere right around here, as I remember."

"Did you really do that?"

"I've done all manner of shit in my day, young lady."

Burl hit the brakes and pulled off the road. "Look," he said, "we've got to get our shit together. This is serious business. It's like an expedition."

"I ain't seen no tornadoes yet," John said. "If you ask me, we should take it slow. It's my day off, and I ain't had any fun yet. Let's take her back to Lawton. I growed up there, you know. I'd like to see some of the scenes of my youth, places where I preached the gospels. Maybe even go up in the Wichita Mountains and take a look at the Holy City."

"Look at that," she said.

It was no more than five miles ahead of them, a long, gray tube silhouetted against the blue rain. They saw it touch the ground: What looked like big sparks shot up as it hit a telephone line.

"Jesus Christ," the girl said.

Then the rain closed in and it was gone. Burl pulled back on the road and stepped on the gas, concentrating on driving as fast as he could.

Ahead he saw the grain elevator at Chattanooga, and a moment later, flashing red lights. There was a highway patrol car parked at the intersection. A mobile home down the street was torn apart. Pink fiberglass insulation was blowing everywhere.

He pulled into the parking lot of the café, where several people were standing around. "You have a twister?" he said, getting out.

"Sure did," one of them said. "Just about five minutes ago. Went through here sounding just like a freight train."

When he went back to the car, she had disappeared again. John rolled down the window.

"Where is she?" Burl asked him.

"In the café."

Burl went inside. Most of the people were looking out the window. The girl was talking to the woman behind the cash register.

"I'm good," she said. "I'm really good. I got clothes, too. These aren't my good clothes. I got caught out in the rain."

"Honey, you'd have to talk to the manager," the woman said, "and I don't think he's gonna be in today."

"I've had a lot of experience. I worked at the Ramada Inn in Oklahoma City. I can give you the name of the person there I worked for."

"You could come back tomorrow," the woman said, not looking at her. "But I don't really think he's looking for anybody. There's three of us, and that's enough to take care of this place."

"Oh all right," she said. "Maybe I'll come back tomorrow." She turned around and saw Burl.

"What are you doing?" he asked her.

"Looking for a job. I just thought they might have a job."

She followed him out into the parking lot.

"Why are you looking for a job here," he asked, "if you live in Lawton?"

"Well, we're not really living in Lawton. We're just

sort of staying at my sister's right now. We're not really living anywhere."

"Look," Burl said, "why don't you just stay here?" He groped in his pocket and pulled out ten dollars. "Here's some money. It's all I've got."

"But there's *nothing* here," she said.

"You can catch a bus or something."

"Look there," she said, pointing to a sign across the road that said LAWTON—30. "It's right down that road. Can't you just take me? My little baby's there."

She was wearing that stupid leather jacket, and she had the same sleepy eyes as the Mexicans in the gondola. Furious, he held open the door for her.

He drove another mile before he saw the big silver vehicles, pulled off by the side of the road ahead. They looked like RVs, but they had strange antennas on top. He had seen them before.

"Who are these fellows?" John said.

"Severe Storms Laboratory."

"You mean they're the big time?"

"That's right," Burl said. "*National Geographic Special* time."

They got out and walked toward a group of scientists and college kids. One kid glanced at Burl, and he had that strange mirrorlike feeling you had when you met someone who looked like you. His hair was almost as long as Burl's and was the same color, but he wore glasses.

"You can't get through," he said. "The power lines are down up ahead."

The kid turned back to the group. Burl moved a little closer, trying to hear what they were saying.

"The Norman Doppler says it's got tops spiking up to sixty thousand feet," one of the scientists said, "and it's got the largest mesocyclone they've ever seen."

"We've been following that storm," Burl said.

The kid glanced at him. "Look, man," he said. "We're busy here. Why don't you take a walk or something?"

The kid turned back to the others. One of them asked him something, and Burl heard him say, "Just a couple of shitkickers."

They walked to the car, Burl's face burning.

"They make you feel like stale beer, don't they?" John said.

"I've seen a few tornadoes," Burl said. "I've probably seen more than they have."

"Don't take it so hard," John said. "They're the big dogs here. They're the professionals. You're just a pup to them."

They got in the Mustang. Burl slammed the door. Then, without knowing he was going to do it, he pulled around the vehicles. They were yelling at him, but he kept right on going. A hundred yards ahead he could see the toppled high tension tower and the cables lying across the road, slithering around just like snakes trying to get close to a rail, for the heat.

"Whoa," John said.

"You're going to kill us," she screamed.

"You wanted to go to Lawton," Burl said. "This is the road to Lawton."

John grabbed him. "I don't know if this is such a good idea."

"No, no," he said, laughing. "The tires will insulate us. We'll be all right." *Unless they touch the gas tank*, he was thinking. If they did, there would be sparks, an explosion.

He felt his asshole pucker as they bumped over the cables, then they were in the clear and picking up speed. "Never again," John was saying, "never again." She was laughing now, handing him the bottle of Herradura, and he took a big gulp.

They followed the storm for another thirty minutes. The clouds were closing in and it was getting dark on the ground. But up there, in the stratosphere, the top of the storm was in full sunlight. It towered like a boiling mountain, glowing white hot. It was the most beautiful storm Burl had ever seen, but it was moving too fast for them. On the radio they heard warnings for it further and further north, until finally even he had to admit they'd lost it. They passed a drive-in movie, and some houses, then they came to a light and he looked ahead and saw neon signs and realized they were already in Lawton.

They went to a place John knew of called the Missile Lounge. She phoned her sister and they sat in a booth, drinking Red Draws, mugs of beer and tomato juice. The place was empty except for two cowboys shooting pool in the back.

"Sorry we didn't catch that tornado," John said.

"That's all right," Burl said. "It was a pretty good day."

The waitress brought John a plate of ribs. John offered Burl some, but he wasn't hungry.

"You don't know what you're missing," John said. "This place has the best ribs in Oklahoma."

Burl was watching the cowboys. It was strange how the weather meant everything to him and nothing to them. To them it was just a rainy afternoon, good for nothing but a game of pool.

She came back and sat down next to John. "How's your baby?" he said.

"She's fine. Look, if you boys are going on, I can hitch a ride from here. One of those cowboys'll probably take me."

"Let's have another beer first," Burl said. He looked at the waitress and held up three fingers.

John offered her a rib. "Want one of these?" he said.

"I've got to tell you something," she said. "When I was on the phone, I looked in the kitchen and saw a colored woman standing barefoot on a pile of those ribs to get something off the shelf."

John looked at the rib. "Probably what gives them flavor," he said, and ate it anyway.

"Well, you're a couple of insane lunatics," she said, "but that was a lot of fun. Next time you decided to go chasing tornadoes, just give me a call."

"Your ol' man might not like that," John said.

"Screw him. He's nothing but trouble. I'm gonna get rid of him. He's got a drug problem."

"So do I," John said. "The railroad won't let me smoke pot. It's a clear violation of my Fourth Amendment rights."

"Well, I got nothing against pot," she said. "But he's on pills. He drinks too much, too."

"Alcohol's a worse addiction than dope," John said. "It's alcohol that really damages people's minds."

"They're all alcoholics in Russia," she said.

A silence came in.

"Did you really play guitar for Uncontrolled Meltdown?" she said. "I thought you guys would be on the cover of *Rolling Stone* by now."

"So did I," Burl admitted.

"Still a living legend in this part of the country, ain't you?" John said.

"More like ancient history."

Another silence came in. John got up and said, "Guess I'll go test my knowledge." He went over to the Computer Trivia game on the bar and dropped in a quarter.

"You married?" the girl said.

Burl shook his head.

"I really love my ol' man," she said. "But he's so hard to live with. He thinks he's radioactive. He used to work at Pantex, up in Amarillo, where they put together atomic bombs. Now he's sure he's got cancer."

"My dad's got cancer," he said. "It's the same kind the president's got."

She finished her beer and smoothed back her hair. "Hey," she said, smiling. "How'd you get started doing this, anyway?"

What could he say that she would understand? That he wanted to get so close to a tornado that he could look up into the mouth of the funnel and live to tell about it? That he was looking for another world, a world of forces so strong that they could bend the air itself into rings hard as steel?

"I don't know," he said. "I just love tornadoes. They're the only thing that really gets my attention."

"You should be a weatherman," she said.

"Yeah, but it's too late for that now," he said. "I mean, times are so hard I can't afford to think about going back to college. I'm doing good just to keep my job."

"My ol' man can't keep a job either," she said.

"We're all gonna be on welfare," he said. "If Reagan gets his way."

"Hey," she said, smiling. "Want to see something funny?" She took a photo out of her purse and gave it to him. He had to look at it for a moment to figure it out. It had been taken at a carnival, in front of a big blown-up cardboard photo of Ronald Reagan smiling at you. She was on her knees in front of him, her hands on his hips, and it looked like she was giving Ronald Reagan a blow job.

113

*   *   *

"You'd better take a look at this," John called from the door.

They stepped out into the parking lot. Everything had changed. The dryline had broken, and there were storms popping up everywhere. But it was the one to the west, silhouetted against the setting sun, that John was talking about. The moment Burl saw it, an electric thrill shot through him. It had that *black energy*.

"Mean-looking little bugger, ain't it?" John said.

It was the best-looking thing he'd seen all day. Isolated cells like that could consume all the heat and moisture for miles around. It was right down Highway 82, and there was a half an hour of daylight left.

"That one's got my name on it," he said.

"Want to go for it?"

He looked at her. "I don't have to be at my sister's for a while yet," she said. "I'll go with you."

They got in the Mustang and headed down 82, Burl doing seventy, eighty miles an hour. It was a race between them, the storm, and the light. The storm was concentrating, getting smaller, hotter, the base knife-sharp. Just when they needed a road to the north, they found one—a park road, leading up into the Wichita Mountains, the little granite hills north of Lawton. "Watch out you don't hit a buffalo," John said. The park was full of them.

In the end, he found himself wishing he'd gotten out of the storm's way. It was dark as night now on the ground. As the boiling black lip of the storm moved over them, he could see nothing but the tops of the trees, tossing in the wind. He stopped the car and they got out. Just as they did, the setting sun broke through under the base, sending out a shaft of incandescent orange light.

"The Holy City," John cried. Burl saw the three crosses on the stony hill in front of them, the buildings of Bethlehem and Jerusalem. The funnel dropped to the ground, connecting sky and earth, no more than a mile to the north. He had never been so close before, but he heard nothing: They were on the wrong side of the circulation somehow. Then he heard the molecules singing in the roof of the car, and an instant later there was a violet flash as a bolt of lightning hit the ground a hundred yards away. He heard it snap as it broke up into beads of plasma, felt his hair stand on end, saw everything frozen forever, every stone and blade of grass, as her hand touched his.

MOON WALKING

When David left his wife, he lost his home. He moved into a one-room apartment in a part of Chelsea he had always thought of as a slum. He had no possessions, not even a television set—someone had broken in and stolen it the first week. He ate frozen dinners and slept alone on a mattress in the middle of the hard, shiny floor.

Sometimes he went back to his old apartment—his wife's apartment now. He still had a key. When he put it in the lock, he felt the same erotic thrill he would have felt entering a stranger's apartment. All traces of his existence were gone. His closet was filled with his daughter's toys. His wife seemed to be enjoying a new popularity: He took telephone messages from strangers who had never heard of him.

By some inexorable law of New York, his wife's career rose and his fell. She was made a creative executive at Channel 13. Meanwhile, David, who was an actor, found himself unable to get a single role. He sat in his apartment, wondering why his agent no longer returned his calls. From his window he could see the welfare hotel across the street, and the bodega on the corner where three towering black prostitutes hung out all night long. One wore a blonde wig and looked a little like Tina Turner. It took him weeks to figure out they were transvestites.

At the end of the first summer he took a job typing files for a doctor at Bellevue Hospital. When he had not gotten a role in eight months, David decided his career was over. He stayed in New York only because his daughter Audrey was there, and on the one night a week that she slept over he could play the role of father.

In September, David's wife enrolled Audrey, who had just turned three, in a daycare center located in the basement of a church on West End Avenue. David insisted on going to the first parent meeting.

They gathered at eight, sitting in a circle of steel folding chairs, under fluorescent light. Half of the parents were black. Most of the white parents were divorced, or in the process of getting one. David's wife refused to sit with him. She joined the other single mothers, sitting on the other side of the circle of chairs.

Rachel, who was in charge of the center, got up and told them of the problems they faced, which were many. The center received small grants from the city and the federal government, but it was always broke. Since the center could not afford a custodian, parents were asked to come in and clean one evening a month. Who would be the first to volunteer?

"I will." David held up his hand, anxious to appear responsible.

Rachel looked at David's wife. "Will you be joining him?"

"Tomorrow's not a good time for me," she said. "Maybe later in the month."

In the end it was decided that David would clean alone. That was fine with him. He didn't like any of these people anyway.

One of the white parents held up her hand. "I want to protest. I have reason to believe the meals being served here are harmful to the children's health."

"If you mean the meals provided by the government," Rachel said, "they're perfectly healthy. They consist of fresh fruits and vegetables, and the children are not given any white sugar."

"No, but they eat with plastic forks and spoons, and plastic has been proven to be a toxic substance."

It was too much trouble to listen. David looked at the finger paintings on the wall, wondering which one might have been done by his daughter.

Rachel brought the meeting to a close. Jugs of cheap white wine were brought out and the parents split into two groups—smokers and non-smokers. David joined the smokers, most of them men. The single mothers watched them from the other side of the room, radiating a contempt that he could almost feel on his face, like heat.

Audrey loved the daycare center, especially the black children, most of whom had African names like Mosi, Ugo, and Shumba. Her best friend was a little girl named Dahlila. In another month, it began to seem to David that his daughter was becoming a little black child herself.

Audrey spent most of every day at the center, from eight-thirty to five-thirty. In the mornings, the children played on the jungle gym in the air shaft. Before lunch, the teacher read them stories in which Grover, Ernie, and Big Bird learned about good nutrition. In the afternoons, if it wasn't too cold, they went to the park. While the children were waiting for their parents to pick them up, the teacher sometimes put on records and they danced. When David arrived one Friday afternoon in October, Audrey and six or seven black children were dancing to "Nasty Boys."

Dahlila's mother was there. She nodded at David—she was one of the few mothers who seemed to like him—and said, "Don't you just love to watch them?"

David had to smile. Audrey was dancing with Dahlila, whose hair was knotted in intricate cornrows, a style Audrey much admired. Like all the black children, Dahlila danced effortlessly. Audrey had all the moves down, but she was trying too hard. Her eyes were full of thought.

"Come on, sugar," he said, when the record ended. "It's time to go."

"Not now, Daddy. I'm having too much fun."

"Daddy's hungry and so are you."

Audrey hugged Dahlila and kissed her good-bye. They had been inseparable ever since Audrey's first day at the center. They held hands everywhere they went, and often whispered secrets in each other's ears.

David led Audrey to the subway and they rode downtown. It was dark when they got to his apartment. Audrey got out her coloring books, while David fixed a dinner of hamburger and frozen peas, which they ate sitting on the floor. "Daddy," she said, "when are you going to get a table?"

"It's more fun this way," he said. "We can pretend we're having a picnic."

"I wish you had a television," she said. "Then I could watch *Fat Albert and the Cosby Kids*."

119

"You shouldn't watch too much television," he said. "It's not good for you."

When he removed her jeans so she could take her bath, he saw, to his horror, that her knees were covered with scabs.

"What happened?" he asked her.

"Ugo pushed me down."

David knew Ugo. He was older than the other children. His mother was white, his father black. His eyes were hot with intelligence and anger. Once he had walked up to David and whispered, *Hello, motherfucker.*

"Ugo's got a bad temper," he said.

"But he's the best dancer. He can moon walk."

"Your mother and I want you to take a real dance class," he said. "We've been talking about it. Then you can wear a leotard and learn ballet, and when you get older, maybe you can be in *The Nutcracker*."

"But I want to learn how to moon walk."

He felt so sorry for her, growing up in this harsh city where she had to play on concrete, with angry boys. She should have had a childhood like his, full of green lawns and friendly dogs.

After her bath, he helped her into her pajamas and read her *The Ugly Duckling*. He was trying to introduce her to the stories of Hans Christian Andersen, although she was too young to really understand them. He hated the *Sesame Street* characters she loved, especially Big Bird, who somehow reminded him of his wife.

"Daddy," she said, "sometime I want to sleep over at Dahlila's."

"Do you?"

"Her mother said she'd do my hair in cornrows."

"That would be nice."

"Daddy, I just love Dahlila *so* much."

"I know, sugar."

"She's my best friend. And she doesn't have a daddy either."

"You have a daddy."

"I know, but you don't live with us. And neither does hers."

When she had fallen asleep, he went into the kitchen and had a drink and a cigarette. He was trying to stop smoking around her—she had already found out about lung cancer.

It was a cold night, but the tenants of the welfare hotel were sitting out on the steps and drinking beer, their ghetto blasters playing loud, metallic rap. David couldn't understand how they could sit out there drinking beer on a cold night like tonight.

But in another way, he understood them better now. For the first time in his life, David knew what it was to be poor. Every week, he went to the *Cambio* in Times Square, where he joined a line of blacks and Puerto Ricans, shoved his paycheck through a bulletproof glass window, and got it back in cash, less five percent. He never saved any money. Spending it was the only thing that could make him feel better. He paid his rent with a money order, and with what was left, bought a bottle of vodka and a meal at the Asia de Cuba, a few blocks away, where they served *comidas, criollas,* and *chinas.* By the end of the week his money was almost gone. Like the tenants of the welfare hotel, he had no past and no future, so he lived in the only place he could—the present.

Of all the things that he had lost, David missed most the comfort of women. He hated living alone. But the women of New York had no interest in a man who was broke. Also, he was divorced, and a divorced man was something to be avoided for several years afterwards, like a nuclear reactor that had suffered a meltdown. He felt fine: But to women, he emitted hot, invisible particles of despair.

Worse, it seemed that he was starting to frighten women. They seemed to sense an anger in him that had not been there before. In December, he forced himself to go to several auditions, including one where he had to threaten a woman with a rubber knife. Just when he thought he was getting to the best part of the scene, the director broke in and said, "Thanks, but you're not what we're looking for." When he handed the script back to the stage manager, he noticed she was trembling.

On Monday afternoon, he finally got hold of his agent. David had originally signed with the hottest agent in New York—a maker of movie stars. In time, his agent had moved out to Hollywood, saying he would send for him. David had been passed down to his assistant; and when he moved on, to *his* assistant.

The agency had gone through an incredible period of expansion, with people being promoted almost every week. Today, three years later, David's original agent headed a movie studio. David was now working with someone who had been in the mail room when he signed on. David was the oldest of his clients. His others, it seemed to David, were more models than actors, and often appeared in the pages of *Interview*.

"How did they like me?" he asked.

His agent sighed. "I hate to tell you this," he said, "but they thought you had an attitude."

"An attitude?"

"You know. They thought you were an asshole."

David tried to think of something to say. If the conversation were to lag even slightly he knew his agent would have, within seconds, another phone call.

"I've been thinking," he said. "What if I went out to California for pilot season?"

"I don't think you're ready to go to California."

"How do you know? You've never seen me work."

"You haven't gotten a job," his agent said. "Not since I've been handling you. You've got to get your name around first. You should do a soap."

"You've got to send me up for a soap."

"Look," his agent said, "I've got another call."

That night, drunk on vodka—it seemed appropriate to drink vodka in this great, cold city that reminded him of his childhood nightmares of Russia, where everyone labored endlessly, and even children had to go to school six days a week—he decided to go down to the bodega for cigarettes. He had only a twenty-dollar bill to get him through the rest of the week. He put it in his pocket, threw on his jacket, and went downstairs.

He walked toward the bodega. He had forgotten his gloves, but he didn't care. Ahead he saw the three black transvestites, thin as walking razors, tall as African tribeswomen in the *National Geographic*. He heard the one who looked like Tina Turner say, "Here he come."

Suddenly they surrounded him, their hands everywhere, passing over his thighs, his groin. He couldn't move. A hand fastened itself to his cock, a pair of lips were at his ear. "Hey, mistah," one said. "You want a blow job?" He heard himself laughing. "Not tonight," he said, trying to sound experienced. "Maybe some other time." He was suffocating in the smell of wine and cheap perfume, but it was the smell of women, and he lingered a little longer. "Please," he said finally. "You've got the wrong guy." Then they were gone, melting away and disappearing up the street. He went into the bodega, thinking of them almost fondly: It had been so long since anyone had thought of him as a sexual prospect, even for money. Not until he reached into his pocket to pay for his cigarettes did he discover the twenty-dollar bill was gone.

There was a pound of hamburger in the refrigerator for Audrey's dinner on Friday night, a jar of peanut butter, and a loaf of bread. If he walked to work, he thought he could make it through the rest of the week.

For the next three days, he lived as he had in college, on peanut butter sandwiches. He drank lots of water— he'd heard water filled you up. After the first day he felt no real hunger, just a mild depression.

The mornings were the worst, but if he drank enough coffee, he could always keep going. By Thursday he had lost five pounds, and his depression had turned into detachment. You're fasting, he told himself. It's good for you.

That night, he went to the daycare center to clean.

"You're late," Rachel said, as he came through the door.

"I'm sorry," he said. "I got held up at the hospital."

"That's all right," she said, suddenly softening. "Here, why don't you have a cup of coffee before you start? You look tired."

She poured him a cup of coffee and he watched her clear her desk of pencils and paper clips.

"How long have you worked at the hospital?" she asked him.

"Since we got divorced," he told her. Then he added, "I'm an actor. But I haven't gotten any parts lately."

"I know," she said. "My husband and I used to go to the theater. I saw you in *Punishment Detail*." She locked her desk drawer. "I thought you were wonderful."

Sometimes, it had seemed to him that the very women

who hated him the most—his wife's friends—lusted after him in secret. Rachel, for instance. Sometimes he had caught her looking at him with a certain appreciation. He was the one who had gotten away. Her own husband, a lawyer, was a thoroughly mild and submissive man who always wore a coat and tie.

"Thanks," he said.

"I was in a few plays in college," she said, smoothing her hair. "Just small parts. Nothing important. But for a while, I thought I wanted to be an actress."

"I'll bet you were pretty good," he told her.

They talked about her favorite actress, Jane Fonda—who, like her, had gone to Vassar—and her favorite performance, Jane Fonda as Bree Daniels in the movie *Klute*—which David could have predicted. Many women her age, he had noticed, loved that character—perhaps because they secretly felt like high-class prostitutes; perhaps because she had the same name as their favorite cheese. She told him they were moving to Israel next year. Her husband's parents lived in Tel Aviv. It had been her idea, but now she wasn't sure she wanted to go.

"What about you?" she said. "Why aren't you out in California? You could probably find work in television."

"Yeah," he said. "But then I couldn't see my daughter."

"I think that's very admirable."

It came to him that they were all alone and had been talking for a long time. The air held a rich odor of interest he associated with an audience that was enjoying a performance. Could it be possible she wanted him? It couldn't—but hadn't he learned and forgotten all over again that whenever you found yourself having stubborn fantasies about a woman, she was having them too?

Rachel suddenly cleared her throat. "Well," she said.

"My husband will be wondering where I am. You'll remember to lock up, won't you?"

He told her he would. They exchanged a last look—a lingering look, it seemed to him—and she left.

David poured Pine-Sol into a bucket and started mopping the floor. He kept going back over the conversation. She had said she found him admirable. The words filled him with a warm glow. Someone admired him. He worked slowly and carefully, trying to hold onto the moment. He pretended he was in the navy. He wished she would come back and see him working. He knew now why he lusted after his wife's friends: He wanted their forgiveness.

Someone had left a carton of milk on the kitchen counter. He opened the refrigerator to put it away. That was when he saw the lunches the Department of Education gave to the center, dozens of little plastic cartons, each one holding a tunafish sandwich, an apple, a hard-boiled egg. Hunger gripped his stomach like a clamp.

No one would ever know. David tore open a carton and bit into an apple. Too late he heard footsteps behind him.

"I forgot something," Rachel said softly.

He turned, his mouth full of apple. "My God," she said. "Stealing the children's food."

Before she slammed the door, she added, "Your wife told me you were a loser. Now I believe it."

On Friday evening, David picked up Audrey and brought her to his apartment. Tomorrow morning, she was going to her first dance class; and tomorrow afternoon was Dahlila's birthday party. It was hard to say which she was more excited about.

While he fixed her dinner, she took off her blue jeans

126

and danced around his apartment in her leotard. "Daddy," she said, "I used to not like your apartment because it didn't have any furniture. But now I do because it's like a dance studio."

David's agent called, just as they sat down to eat dinner. As usual he spoke rapidly, producing a smooth, transparent stream of words that seemed to gush from the phone like water from a hose. It took David a moment to understand he was being invited to the agency Christmas party.

"It starts at one o'clock tomorrow afternoon," his agent was saying. "There'll be some people here I think you should meet." He named several prominent lesbian casting directors.

They must have been planning this for months, David thought. Why didn't I get an invitation?

"I didn't ask you before because I know how you hate these things," his agent was saying. "You're not a social person."

"Will there be food?" David asked.

"Of course there'll be food," his agent said. "Can you be here?"

"I'll come after I drop off my daughter," David said.

"Oh, and David. Wear something nice. Try not to look like you just crawled out of a boxcar."

David looked in the closet. Fortunately he had a clean shirt. He thought he could get by.

After Audrey's bath, he put her to bed and read her *The Little Match Girl*. As he finished, his eyes filled with tears.

"You're crying, Daddy," she said.

"That story always makes Daddy cry," he said. "It's good to cry sometimes. Next week, I'll read you the story of *The Little Fir Tree*. It's about a little tree that got to be a Christmas tree.''

"Are you going to have a Christmas tree?"

"If you want one."

"There's not much room," she said.

"Daddy doesn't need that much room. He lives by himself."

He turned off the light and pulled the covers up around her chin.

"Daddy," she said, "I'm afraid to go to Dahlila's."

"Why?"

"Because she told me there's a cemetery near her house, and sometimes at night skeletons come out of it, just like in 'Thriller.' "

"Dahlila says a lot of things. She's just making that up. You don't believe her, do you?"

"Daddy, I'm afraid I'm going to have a nightmare."

"No you're not," he said. "I'll see you have good dreams tonight."

He went into the kitchen and poured himself a drink.

"Daddy?" she said from the other room.

"Yes, sugar?"

"Why can't I come live with you?"

"Because you'd miss Mommy if you lived with me."

"Why can't you and Mommy live together?"

"Because we made each other unhappy."

He waited for her to say something else, but she didn't, and after a while he went in and could tell by her breathing she was asleep. She coughed, and he put his hand on her forehead. It felt hot. She seemed to always have colds now.

She was slipping away from him, into another, harsher world. And she was growing so fast now. He remembered the time when she had started daycare, only four months

128

ago. She had still been a baby then. Sometimes he had carried her the eight blocks home on his back because she was too tired to walk. Stop spoiling her, his wife had scolded him. But he had enjoyed it. They had stopped half-way there, sat on the steps of a brownstone, and talked. Daddy, she had asked him, puzzled about the slogan of a local bank, what does it mean, *the road to riches starts at the Dime?* And he had tried to explain to her, answering question after question until he found himself describing the whole world. This was Manhattan, that was New Jersey, that thing in the sky was the moon. It was like another country, where no one lived, and it was far away, higher than an airplane could fly. "Carry me, Daddy," she had said, putting her arms around his neck. "Carry me to the moon."

When he woke, Audrey was standing at the window. "Daddy, get up," she said. "I'm afraid we're going to miss class."

The sky was gray, the streets still. He looked at the clock. It was seven-thirty. "We've still got three hours," he told her.

"Daddy," she said. "Please."

He got up, made her a bowl of cereal, himself a cup of instant coffee. Then he took a bath, shaved, and put on his clean shirt. He needed a haircut, but there was nothing he could do about that.

It was a cold, clear day. The night's urine had frozen to the sidewalk, ribbons of yellow ice. They rode the subway uptown to 72nd Street and walked to the dance studio, on the second floor of a building just off West End Avenue. David pressed the intercom button, identified himself, and they were let in.

They climbed a flight of stairs and found themselves in a little lobby with a desk. Behind it sat an older woman, her gray hair pulled back into a bun. The walls were covered with posters of famous dance companies.

"Are we late?" he said.

"No, you're the first ones. The dressing room's at the end of the hall."

Holding Audrey's hand, he led her down the hall. The entrance to the dressing room was covered with a curtain. He shoved it aside and they entered a small room with lockers around the walls that smelled of sweat and cosmetics. He helped Audrey remove her jeans and pull on her pink leotard.

When they came out, two other little girls were just arriving with their mothers. They ran screaming into the studio, a mirrored room whose floor was covered with gray linoleum, and threw themselves on a pile of gym mats.

"Don't you want to go in there?" he asked Audrey, who had gone limp against his leg and was sucking her thumb.

"Not yet, Daddy."

David had wanted to stay, but now he felt uncomfortable. The dance studio gave him the same uncomfortable feeling he'd had as a child, when his mother had led him through the ladies' lingerie section of the department store.

He took a cigarette out of his pocket. The gray-haired woman wordlessly pointed to a sign that said THANK YOU FOR NOT SMOKING and he dropped it into a coffee can full of sand.

"Audrey," he said, "I've got to go."

He started back down the hall to the dressing room, where he had left his bag. When he shoved the curtain aside, there was a young woman standing in the middle of the room—a beautiful young woman with a dancer's body who had to be the teacher. She stopped, frozen in the act of pushing down her top, one lovely breast exposed.

"Sorry," he said, feeling blood rush to his face. He went back down the hall.

Audrey had joined the other little girls in the dance studio. He stood there for a moment, his upper lip covered with perspiration. He needed to get out of there, but he had to tell Audrey good-bye. He looked into the studio, and to his surprise saw a strange man glaring angrily at him. *Who is that guy?* he thought. *Whoever he is, he looks dangerous.* A moment later he realized it was his reflection in one of the mirrors.

He turned back. The teacher was standing only inches away from him, her hands on her hips, a furious expression on her face. She turned to the woman at the desk. "That's him," she said. "That's the same guy who followed me here last week." She turned back to David. "Get off on watching little girls, do you?"

"I think he's a parent," the woman said.

"Call the police," the teacher said.

The woman had gotten up. "No," she was saying. "I think he's a parent. He brought a little girl here."

"I don't care who you are," the teacher said, picking up the phone. "I'm calling the police."

"Good-bye, Audrey," David called out, as he went through the door and stumbled down the stairs to the street.

He sat down on the curb for a moment, trying to catch his breath. When he looked up, he saw his wife coming toward him.

"What are you doing here?" she said.

"I got thrown out."

"Why?"

"I don't know," he said. "Something about me seems to bother women."

"Probably because you're so hostile," she said. "Look, I've got to talk to you."

They went to a luncheonette, took a booth, and ordered two cups of coffee. "All right," he said. "What is it?"

"Don't be hard on me," she said. "I'm not feeling very together right now. I got mugged last night."

"Jesus," he said. "How did it happen?"

"I was going to a party, on Riverside Drive. It was only three blocks, so I thought I'd walk. This kid came out of Riverside Park and showed me a knife and told me to give him my purse."

"Did he hurt you?"

"No, but I lost two hundred dollars."

"You're lucky you didn't get hurt."

"I know," she said, "but I'm very upset. I couldn't sleep at all last night. So you're going to have to take Audrey to Dahlila's birthday party."

"But I *can't*," he said.

"You don't want to disappoint her, do you? You know how much this means to her."

He told her about his agent's Christmas party. "I've got to go. It might mean work. Are you sure you can't take her?"

"David, the party's in the South Bronx. You know what it's like up there. A white woman was killed up there last week. Nobody's going to bother you. You're too big."

"The other night," he said, "I got robbed by three homosexuals. And they weren't even carrying a knife."

"David," she said hotly, "you've been no help to me. You never give me any money. I've had to do everything for her myself. Well, you can start helping now."

He toyed with a coat button, sick with the effort of trying to keep control. Women could get as angry as they wanted. An angry woman was only being assertive. But an angry man was guilty of the worst male sin.

"All right," he said, finally. "I'll take her."

The cab driver said, when he gave him the address, "Forget it, buddy. I can't go up there. Can't get a fare back." The party would start in fifteen minutes, so he led Audrey to the subway and they boarded an uptown train.

They rode north. One by one, the other white people got off. The stations were dirtier, the walls covered with posters for Sta Fro and Afro Sheen. David concentrated on Audrey. When he looked up again, there were only three other people in the car—a young black couple with a baby carriage, and a black kid drinking a Yoo Hoo. Three black toughs strode through the car, looking left and right. Like the other passengers, David stared at the floor, feeling their eyes pass over him.

Somewhere beyond the Grand Concourse, the train emerged from the tunnel. Sunlight flooded in. He saw a fence of corrugated sheet iron, topped by coils of barbed wire. He felt they were entering a concentration camp. Looking out, he saw a brilliant blue sky full of flying clouds. On the ground—desolation. There were hills of brown dirt, dead trees, lots full of broken pink brick. A few abandoned buildings towered over it all like great tombstones, their windows covered with tin. The train floated as if in a dream above what looked like the ruins of Berlin, Stalingrad, the wheels screaming as they slowly rounded a curve and pulled into an elevated station.

They got off, the doors shut, and the train moved away. Holding Audrey's hand, David looked around. Below, a single inhabited street slanted through the rubble. In the remote distance, he saw the Empire State Building. Giving it a last look, he led Audrey down the wooden steps.

They walked uphill, past Paco's Discount and the Iglesia Pentacostal. He saw a dog pulling at a plastic garbage bag, a drunk in a doorway whose sagging pants had partially exposed his buttocks. At the top of the hill were two project buildings, with a courtyard between.

"It's cold, Daddy," said Audrey. Even she seemed to sense they did not belong here.

"We'll be there soon," he said, looking at the address. They crossed the courtyard, their shoes crunching on broken glass, and entered a lobby painted industrial green. He pressed the intercom button. No reply. It was broken.

They climbed eight flights of stairs, through the strong metallic odor of cockroaches, and knocked on the door. It opened with a burst of noise and motion, and instantly what seemed like a whirlwind of six or seven black children spun out. *Audrey!* they shouted. *Audrey's here!* They were all around David, touching him, pulling at his coat. "Hey, mistah," one said. "You Audrey's daddy?" He nodded, not knowing what to say. Then Audrey had been caught up and spun away. He caught a glimpse of her disappearing into a bedroom down the hall, a bedroom full of black children jumping up and down on a bed, throwing pillows. Then Dahlila's mother was smiling at him and holding out her hand. "I'm so glad you could come," she said. "So glad." He let her take his coat. "Come in here," she said, "and meet everybody."

His heart was thudding. He felt light as air as he let

her lead him into the living room, where several grown-
ups were watching television. A very old man with a
cane, his face finely seamed and polished, stood when
David was introduced and offered his papery dry hand,
nodding with infinite gravity. He was also introduced to a
woman wearing a glossy black bouffant wig and a young
man who smiled shyly. He sat down, still feeling weight-
less, on the green sofa next to the old man. His eyes
found the only other white face in the room—the image of
Howard Cosell on the television screen—and for a long
time, that was the only face he could look at.

Then Dahlila's mother touched his shoulder and said,
"You look like you could use something to eat." When he
nodded, she brought him a plate of chicken wings and a
glass of wine punch. The saliva rushing into his mouth
was actually painful, like the stab of a knife. He ate
several chicken wings and had three glasses of punch.
The young man offered him a Kool. He found he was able
to look around the room. There was a feeling here, com-
pounded by the presence of the old man, the way everyone was watching television but talking to each other now
and then, the way they ignored the shouting and laughter
of the children in the other room. It was the feeling of a
family.

"Did you have any trouble getting here?" Dahlila's
mother asked.

"Trouble?" he said. "No, we didn't have any trouble."

"Dahlila was afraid Audrey wouldn't come," she
said. "But I told her, don't you worry. Her daddy's not
going to let her miss your party."

The cake was brought out and the children rushed in,
their laughter filling the room as if with light. The candles
were blown out, Dahlila tore open her packages, and
everyone had a piece of cake. Then Dahlila's mother put

on a record and all the children danced. "Look, Daddy," Audrey cried. "I'm moon walking." He nodded, then looked away before she saw his eyes fill with hot, rushing tears of pure joy.

THE DESERT

My father was a petroleum geologist. Today, they've got a lot of help—they look for oil with dynamite charges and geophones, exploding the charges and recording the shock wave as it moves through the layers of rock. Then this information goes into a computer.

But my father didn't have all this technology. He studied the surface formations. From what he could see, he tried to imagine what he could not. Slowly, he built up a picture of the landscape as it had existed through time, layer after layer for millions of years.

When he thought he'd found oil, he told them where to drill. Sometimes he was right, and sometimes wrong. But people thought he was good—some people thought he was the best geologist they'd ever worked with.

We lived in Texas, but his early jobs took us all over the country. As he drove, he pointed out geologic features. Other families looked at landmarks from the history of the United States; we looked at landmarks from the history of the world. When I was six years old, we drove to Wyoming in a yellow Chrysler. I rode in the backseat, too little to understand much of what my parents said. But I knew we were happy—my father because he had a good job, my mother because now we could buy a house, and me because on the radio Vaughn Monroe was singing my favorite song, "Ghost Riders in the Sky."

It got dark. Then, fifty miles ahead, we saw a light. When we got closer, it was a big yellow torch.

"A rig's on fire," my father said.

He pulled off the road to get a closer look and lifted me onto the hood of the Chrysler. The air trembled, and I could feel heat on my face.

He explained how oil was found in underground pools. Something had ignited the oil, and now it might burn for months. But won't it all burn up? I wanted to know.

"Yes, Sonny," my father said. "Someday it will all be gone."

At first I thought of my father as a soldier. When I was very young, he showed me a photograph of himself, wearing a helmet and fatigues, holding a machine gun, and standing in front of his jeep, somewhere in Belgium.

He was there when Patton's Third Army relieved the airborne at the Battle of the Bulge; he crossed the Remagen Bridge three days after it was captured and helped trap the German Army in the Ruhr Pocket. He was a captain and avoided General Patton, who was hard on officers. Once, when Patton arrived at a farmhouse command post, my father, along with several other officers, climbed out a rear window. He brought back a Bronze Star, his decoration for valor, a Nazi ceremonial dagger, and a pistol taken from a German prisoner. Sometimes he brought his footlocker down from the attic and I was allowed to look at these things. The Bronze Star was in a blue plush case. The dagger had a chrome blade. Best of all was the pistol, black and deadly.

Then something went wrong. My father changed. He got frighteningly angry for reasons I couldn't understand, and I fell out of love with him. Suddenly he seemed to have a lot of enemies. Every night he watched the Army–McCarthy hearings on television. "Maybe old Georgie Patton was right," he said. "When we finished with the Germans, we should have taken on the Reds."

He became very suspicious. There were floodlights in our backyard so he could cook outside. Sometimes, without warning, he would turn them on.

"What's wrong?" I would say.

"Nothing. I just thought I heard somebody in the backyard."

For years my father went along, never earning much money. Meanwhile, his friends were making their pile, moving into big offices downtown and hiring younger geologists to work for them.

Then he did make money. He found an overlooked deposit of oil only thirty miles away. It was brilliant geology. Everyone said so. But instead of moving downtown, my father built an office in the garage. Money bought freedom, but what did he do with it? He bought a big Steinway piano.

My father loved the piano. As a boy in Lincoln, Nebraska, he had taught himself to play; had earned pocket money in high school by playing for a movie theater that still showed silent pictures. Now he practiced all the time. Instead of making more money, he learned to play Chopin.

But it got so I hated to come home and hear him playing. It meant he'd been drinking. Sometimes I would go in his office and look at his maps. Before he made money, he had spent long hours working on them. Each contour line was lovingly inked in; there were overlays of colored tissue paper for each geologic age. Now they were ignored.

My father was trying to decide what to do. He thought about it longer and longer, staying up all night at the piano and sleeping all day.

Once, when he was cleaning the pistol, my mother said it was dangerous and he should throw it away. To prove that an unloaded pistol was not dangerous, my father aimed it out the back door and pulled the trigger. The bullet made a small hole in the screen.

When my father was in his early forties, he began doing field work again. That summer he took us to Chambers, Arizona. There was no town, just the yellow cinderblock motel, where we lived, in the middle of nowhere. Ten miles west was the Painted Desert. Across the highway was the Navajo Reservation.

Every morning my father's Navajo driver knocked on the door of my parents' room. He drove my father off into the desert, leaving my mother and me behind. While she read the *Ladies' Home Journal* under the roaring air-conditioner, I watched the other guests leave. Most were on their way to California. Night had surprised them on this long, empty stretch between Gallup and Flagstaff. They got in late and left early the next day.

Sometimes I walked around behind the motel, where a big landfill, full of garbage, sloped down to the Puerco River. A girl stood in the back door of the café adjoining the motel. She was a year or so older than I was. "What's your name?" she said.

"Bill."

"Where you from, Billy?"

"Texas." I tried to sound tough. Girls who called you Billy didn't take you seriously.

"I got a horse. Maybe we can ride it sometime."

"Maybe."

She disappeared into the cafe. Then I walked along the highway, past the corral and her horse and an old Airstream trailer, my loafers filling with hot sand.

I was fourteen years old. My grades were not very good. I sketched in my notebook instead of writing down the things my teachers said. When I was younger, I had suffered from terrifying nightmares about the atomic bomb. I had seen our house, standing alone in the Nevada desert like the houses on the television programs. There was a flash, and the shingles ignited; then there was only flying debris as the shock wave rolled over it, like surf.

"Learn everything about what frightens you," my father had said, "and you can overcome it." I had taken his advice and had learned everything there was to know about protons, neutrons, electrons. The nightmares had stopped. Now I had only one problem—talking to girls.

Ahead, I heard singing. Three Navajos sat under a highway bridge. They wore robes and big hats and passed a bottle. There was a fire, the flames almost invisible in the glare. The singing faded in and out as the wind shifted. I crouched down and watched them for a long time.

Later, when they were gone, I went closer. Empty bottles of Gallo Thunderbird lay on the sand. I poked the ashes of the fire with a long stick. What sort of people, I wondered, would sit around a fire on a day like this, drinking, wearing those hot clothes? A big semi boomed over the bridge. I got nervous and walked back to the motel.

My father returned about the time the neon sign out front began to glow. He wore a clean white shirt to dinner, and a string tie with a turquoise clasp. After closing time, the couple who owned the motel sat in our booth and talked to my parents. Everyone was friendly here. I watched their daughter, whom I'd spoken to that morning, working in the kitchen with two Navajo girls. Later, her boyfriend came for her in a pickup. Wearing charcoal-gray slacks, a pink shirt, and a thin gray plastic belt, I dropped nickel after nickel in the jukebox, playing a song I didn't even like, Pat Boone's "Love Letters in the Sand."

From the day we came to Chambers, we heard about Hank Luscombe, who ran the trading post—he had lived with a Navajo woman, had tried peyote. He sounded like the most interesting person around. One evening, my father and I drove over to see him.

The trading post was on the old, bypassed highway, a mile north. It was a long, low building, part log, part adobe. Navajos sat on the front porch, ignoring us and drinking Orange Crush.

Hank had a sly, dishonest look. As he talked to my father, his eye kept roving around and finding me. I felt uncomfortable and walked away through rooms that got smaller and smaller. In the last room of all, I found the paintings.

They were of birds, deer, Navajo. Painted in bright primary colors, they showed a world of stylized light. The moon was a silver crescent, the clouds a glowing, scalloped line. The most beautiful, to my mind, was of an impossibly blue horse.

"You buy?"

A big Navajo was standing at my shoulder, his hair in a pigtail. "Fifty dollars," he said.

Hank, followed by my father, came into the room. "This is Jimmy Begay," he said. "He painted all those pictures."

"Fifty dollars. Good price."

"We're not looking for a painting," my father said.

"Hank," the Navajo said, "you got something for me?"

They went in the other room. Through the window, a moment later, we watched him leave. In one hand he carried a can of tomatoes; in the other, a bottle wrapped in a paper sack.

Hank returned and told us about Jimmy Begay. He had joined the Marines at fourteen, lying about his age. When he came back, he started to paint. Among collectors of Indian art he was famous; but he hadn't sold a major painting for two years.

"I thought liquor was illegal on the reservation," my father said.

"I give Jimmy a bottle now and then. He does me a favor, bringing me those paintings, so I do him one. Jimmy's my friend."

He showed us the largest one—a Navajo in a Marine uniform, floating in a thundercloud and staring off over golden mesas with a look of tragic, helpless love.

"He says this is his masterpiece. But he wants five hundred dollars for it, and it's so gloomy nobody will buy it."

Hank was right. Nobody ever bought the painting. But I was inspired and began sketching the horse in the corral behind the motel. This should have been easy, since it stood motionless for hours. Sometimes I almost got the proportions right. But I always gave up and went back to my room. The motel was silent at noon except for the droning, singsongy chants on Radio Gallup, which I could half hear on the maid's transistor radio. Under my bed I kept a copy of *Playboy* I had found on the landfill. It was years old, but its pages had been preserved by the dry desert air. I stared at it for hours. There was one photograph of Marilyn Monroe, her skin the color of honey, lying naked on a spill of red velvet. Sometimes it seemed afterwards I had actually made love to her.

One Saturday we drove to Gallup. While my parents went shopping, I went to see a movie I'd heard a lot about, *Rebel Without a Cause.*

For two hours, I became the boy on the screen—had a knife fight, wore a red nylon windbreaker, screamed at my parents, *You're tearing me apart*, tried to save Plato by emptying his gun of shells. When I came out, I stared into the blue mirror covering the facade of the building next door and was shocked to see I was still myself. Staring back was the same confused face of my yearbook photo.

The building was a hock shop. I went inside and bought a switchblade with a transparent handle—when it was turned just the right way, you could see a naked girl, her pubic hair covered by the ace of spades.

All the way back to Chambers, I stared out the car window, having grim, enjoyable visions of being misunderstood for the rest of my life. "What's wrong with you?" my mother said.

"Nothin'," I mumbled.

"For God's sake, Sonny, speak up!" my father said. "I can't understand a word you're saying."

But I didn't answer. I was busy perfecting my impersonation of James Dean, teenager from the moon.

After dinner that night, I sat at the counter, rolling one toothpick after another out of the dispenser, until the girl leaned across the Formica top and said, "Billy, is something wrong?"

"No," I said, rolling out another toothpick.

"Come back in the kitchen, so we can talk."

I followed her. She wore a papery skirt and shoes with red crepe soles. The Navajo girls dropped silverware and giggled at us. "Billy," she said with some concern, "are you In Trouble?"

This was the fifties, and being In Trouble could mean anything from being pregnant to stealing hubcaps. I made up a story on the spot, borrowing from the movie. "I go to a pretty tough school. They get rough with you if you don't belong. . . . Sometimes they fight with knives. If you don't they think you're chicken."

I showed her my knife. She seemed to like what she heard. The movie had confirmed something I had long suspected: Girls didn't go for nice guys. They liked the guys who got In Trouble; liked the guys they said they didn't like.

"Let's go out to my uncle's trailer," she said. "He's got a radio."

Her uncle was a ham operator. The walls of the trailer were covered with postcards. She tuned his big Zenith to a commercial station, and from far-off Chicago I heard the Coasters singing "Searchin'." "Come on," she said, holding out her hand, "pretend I'm your big sister."

"I don't feel like it."

I looked instead at postcards from Dayton, Ohio, and Anchorage, Alaska. Most of my dancing had been done with myself, in front of a mirror. Dancing with a girl seemed almost as impossible as going all the way with her.

"You are a strange boy. I watch you sometimes. What are you doing out there all day long?"

"Sketching."

"You going to be an artist?"

"Maybe."

"Dancing's against our religion," she said. "We're Latter-Day Saints. But sometimes my boyfriend takes me. The Navajo girls showed me some steps."

She opened a cabinet. Inside was a bottle. "Maybe someday I'll stop going to church, like my uncle did. He drinks and plays poker all night long with his railroad friends. "Say," she said, looking at me, "how about drinking some of this?"

My mouth had the metallic taste that goes along with doing all dangerous things for the first time; but there was never any doubt I was going to drink it.

After we had some, she took the bottle to the sink. "I'll just put some tap water in it and he'll never know the difference," she said. "It's always worked before." She left the bottle on the table.

Together we sat on the couch, and she told me about going to Gallup with her boyfriend. "Maybe you and me can drive to Gallup sometime."

"I can't. I mean, my parents took away my license when I got In Trouble."

We had another one. I thought it was doing nothing to me and wondered why my father liked it. While we talked she extended one leg, pointing it at the bottle, dangling her shoe from one toe like a little girl. I got up to put the bottle away, but found myself in the bathroom, staring at my reflection in the dirty mirror. Did my face show any change? My lips no longer had any feeling in them.

Now the Five Satins were singing a sad, ghostly song,

"In the Still of the Night." "Won't you try dancing with me?" she said. "Just once."

I held her, no big sister now, and we circled slowly on the linoleum floor, grains of sand scratching underfoot. Dancing was easier than I'd thought. I just shifted my weight from one foot to the other.

"You got a girlfriend?"

"Yeah, she's the only one who really understands me."

"What's she look like?"

"I can't describe her. There's this big ol' haunted house, and we go there sometimes and pretend our parents are dead, and we're all we've got."

"You're so strange, Billy."

"Don't call me Billy."

"Bill, Billy," she said. "Who cares? There's billions of Bills, a billion boys."

Silence fell, full of the singing of blood in my ears. Then the screen door was jerked open. I was grabbed and thrust outside; I fell on my hands and knees. I heard a slap; then she ran past me, sobbing. "You've been drinking," her father said to me, righteous as Charlton Heston in *The Ten Commandments*.

"Nosir."

"Don't nosir me. The bottle's right there on the table."

He shoved me along to the door of my parents' room and knocked. The door opened. There they were. "They were dancing," he said, "and drinking her uncle's liquor."

"You don't have to get rough with the boy," my father said apologetically. "I'll discipline him myself."

"See that you do."

The door slammed behind me. My mother said, "You have disappointed me today in more ways than one."

She opened my door, and to my horror I saw the

Playboy lying on the bed. The maid must have left it there when she made up my room.

My father was taking off his belt. "I haven't punished you like this since you were a boy," he said, "but I guess you need it."

There was only one thing to do. Screaming, *You're tearing me apart*, I ran off into the night.

For hours I sat on the landfill. There was no place else to go, although I considered hopping a freight to Los Angeles. Secretly, I was very proud of myself. With a long stick I wrote several Love Letters in the Sand. When my parents' lights went out, I slipped back into my room and my bed, trying not to think about tomorrow.

From a great distance, I heard a groaning sound. Struggling up out of sleep, I realized somebody was trying to start my father's Jeep.

Just as I got to the window, my father burst from the door of their room, wearing only Jockey shorts, pistol in hand, and fired into the air.

The shots woke the whole motel. Whoever was trying to steal the Jeep ran off. My father called the police. Sleep was impossible. We sat around in bathrobes. At least my trouble was forgotten.

"I've wished a thousand times you'd throw that old thing away," my mother said.

"If I hadn't had the pistol," my father said, "I would have lost the Jeep."

At daybreak, the Navajo tribal police brought back my father's driver, who had tried to hot-wire the Jeep. They'd caught him hitchhiking, miles down the highway. My father talked to them, then walked away from their car, whose spinning red lights lit up the courtyard. "I didn't press charges," he said. "That boy wasn't worth a goddamn. A year in jail's not going to make him any better."

For a moment he sat, his head in his hands, then looked up. "Sonny, I've got to finish this job, and I don't want to hire another Navajo. Do you think you can help me?"

"Yessir."

"Then I'll give you another chance."

In the desert, I fell back in love with my father. The first day we gassed up at Hank's trading post. I heard a Navajo say, "Where are you going in that Jeep?" It was Jimmy Begay.

"Over toward Black Knoll," my father said, "looking for oil."

"You got a cigarette?" My father gave him one of his Viceroys and they looked at each other.

"You'll get lost out there."

"I don't think so," my father said.

"You be careful, you get lost." He added something in Navajo, and the Indians on the porch laughed. Then he walked off down the road to Wide Ruins.

My father and I drove south, across the Puerco River, onto a ranch belonging to Mr. Paulson. Ahead was a frozen sea—not of ice but of bentonite, yellow desert clay.

My father had to know the elevation of certain beds. He drove me to the foot of a hill and dropped me off. Then I climbed to the top, carrying the surveyor's rod that unfolded in sections, like a carpenter's rule.

Holding the rod upright, I stared off into a world of silent light. To the west was Black Knoll; to the south, the shimmering outline of the White Mountains, fifty miles off. To the east, I could see the tiny figure of my father. He stared back at me through the telescopic sight of his transit, which was mounted on a tripod that stood by the Jeep.

Finally, he walked away from the tripod, waving his hat; a moment later, I heard a faint cry. This was the signal that he was finished. Folding the rod, I climbed down and waited for him to pick me up.

One afternoon at the end of the first week, I noticed my father was in pain. He had injured his back jumping into a ditch in Belgium under fire, and it had given him trouble ever since. "Sonny," he said, "why don't you drive?"

"Are you serious?"

"Go ahead, it's about time you learned."

So I drove the thirty miles back to the motel, learning to coordinate clutch and gas pedal. Maybe that was when I began to love my father again. Knowing I could drive, I looked forward to going back to school in September and perhaps getting my beginner's license, so I could take the car on dates.

In the desert, we told time by light. In the morning, the rocks were pink and gray. At noon, when the sun was overhead, they looked white as plaster. The heat was too great to work. My father parked the Jeep in the shade of a cedar, and we ate lunch.

Then, while he took a nap, I explored the nearby arroyos, keeping my eyes to the ground, looking for pottery left by the tribe the Navajo called the Anasazi, or Old Ones.

As I walked, I thought of the first time my father had taken me into the country. That summer in Wyoming, when I was six years old, we had driven across the prairie, pronghorn antelope scattering from the Jeep. In an arroyo like this, he had found two stones, covered with tiny cracks, and placed then in my hands.

"They're dinosaur eggs," he said. "They've been here so long they've turned to stone."

This country, he told me, was the greatest in the world for fossils. Back there, along the ridgeline, he'd found the thighbone of a brontosaurus.

Couldn't we go get it, take it home? I thought it must be very valuable and was in agony, afraid somebody else would find it.

"They'd walk right past it and not even notice," he said, laughing. "They wouldn't know what to look for." That was the day I had learned what a geologist did.

I liked the way my father looked at this country. Sitting on a petrified log, holding the map on his knees, he stared off at the exposed layers of sandstone: Kayenta, Kaibab, Coconino, Chinle: My father was seeing the memory of the earth.

At the top of the arroyo, I looked out over the whole bentonite sea. After a long time I let my eyes fall on my father sleeping by the Jeep, seemingly at my feet. I had never seen him so happy. In the desert, my father never drank, never wondered what to do. He belonged there.

Later, the light changed again, and the rocks were golden-looking, almost soft. I climbed down the arroyo to wake my father. But he was up before I reached him, as if even in his sleep he had sensed the change. Then we worked another range of hills, until we lost the light entirely.

Once, he dug a bit of yellow rock out from under a ledge with his pocketknife, and I asked him what it was.

"Carnotite. A not-very-pure sample of uranium ore."

"Can't we stake a claim or something?"

151

"No, there's nothing here. The big beds are across the highway, on the Navajo Reservation."

"Well, then, let's go there."

"Even if you found it, it would belong to the Navajos."

I put the rock in the knapsack. "Let's look around," I said. "Maybe there's more."

For a moment I was angry again. This was like the dinosaur bone: another example of my father's knowledge that he could not, or somehow refused to, profit by.

In August, Clint Yarborough came, my father's boss, landing his Beechcraft Bonanza on the dirt strip behind the trading post. He was a gray-haired, handsome man who wore a beautifully tailored blue suit and cowboy boots. When my father showed him the map, he said, "I don't see the structure."

"Right here, along this bed."

"Forget it, you're the geologist. Come on, I'll take y'all to dinner."

Afterwards, back in my parents' room, he propped his expensive boots on the desk. He was paying the bills. "Boy," he said, "why don't you get some ice?" He opened his suitcase and took out a bottle of Wild Turkey.

My father talked geologic theory. "Clint, there's no doubt about it, the younger geologists are right. The continents are in motion."

"I hope Africa doesn't float up next to Padre Island. I got some property there."

My mother forced a laugh, and I hated Clint Yarborough.

"No, Clint, I'm talking about millions of years—"

"Millions? What kind of football team are the Longhorns going to have next year, that's all I care about. You're going to join us for the Cotton Bowl, aren't you? I got a suite at the Adolphus Hotel. You can play the piano

152

and tell all your good stories. Goddamn, you tell a better story than Arthur Godfrey, you know that?"

I went to my room. Later, listening through the walls, I heard Clint say, "People back in North Texas say you're the best geologist there is. They also say you got a drinking problem."

"It's not a problem, Clint, so long as I don't drink."

"You had some tough experiences in the war. That probably had something to do with it. But that's none of my business. I'm proud to employ you."

"Thanks, Clint."

"There's only one thing I want to know: Have we got a well here or not?"

A long silence.

"Just give me your professional opinion."

"You've got a well. The question is, where?"

"All right," Clint said. "When you're absolutely certain, you give me the word. Can you do that?"

"Can do."

"Good." I heard Clint get to his feet. "When it comes in, I'll put you on salary. There's going to be some government reserves turned over to private corporations soon, and Lyndon's a good friend of mine. Yarborough Oil is going places . . . and you could be going places with it."

My father worked more slowly after that. In his silences, as he stared off at the distant beds, I sensed confusion.

One day, there was a thunderstorm. I watched the clouds carefully—the surveyor's rod could attract lightning. From the Jeep my father and I watched the gray broom of rain hitting the desert floor, one hundred, then only fifty yards away. Solid drops struck the roof of the Jeep, like shot. The arroyos were filled with floodwater

153

that looked like moving concrete. Afterwards, the desert was not a world of light but was all in tones of gray, like a photograph. The clouds pressed right down on our heads. The crows always seemed bolder on days like that; they followed us, silently, everywhere we went.

"There's nothing more to do today," my father said. "Let's go home."

Driving back, I decided to take a shortcut up one of the arroyos. My father didn't think I could do it. "The hell I can't," I said.

Halfway up, I got stuck. The Jeep rocked back and forth, wheels spinning in the wet sand. My father told me to get out and push. Nothing worked. Finally, he turned off the ignition.

"We'll walk," he said.

"Walk?"

"Do you want to spend the night here? The road runs right along the top of this arroyo. It's only about seven miles. Here, you take the knapsack."

At the top of the arroyo, we walked through big boulders. "You couldn't have gotten through here anyway," he said. "I shouldn't have let you try. Here's the road. Put a pebble in your mouth."

"What for?"

"So you won't get thirsty."

We walked. At first, I went ahead. When I got a blister and slowed down, my father caught up with me. "What's your hurry?" he said. He took the knapsack. At sunset the sky cleared, and every little stone cast a pencil of violet shadow. Then the sun was gone, and the air was losing its warmth.

At the Puerco Ford, my father was far ahead. He stopped. Against the afterglow, he looked like a silhouette cut out of blotting paper. When I reached him, I said, "What's wrong?"

"There's a fire."

Just ahead was a sandstone outcrop. It was full of caves, hollowed by the wind out of solid rock. Their roofs were blackened by the smoke of countless campfires, their walls scratched everywhere with the petroglyphs of the Anasazi.

Sitting in one were three Navajos. They were drinking Thunderbird around a fire they'd built with one of Mr. Paulson's fenceposts.

"You get lost?" one said. It was Jimmy Begay.

"No," my father said. "We're not lost."

"Come over here and give me a cigarette."

To the north, I could see the lights of the motel. "We're almost home," I said. "It's only another mile or so." But my father sat down by the fire. "That feels good," he told them. "We were getting cold."

He passed around cigarettes; they offered him the bottle, but he refused. "What are you looking for out there?" Jimmy said.

"Oil."

"There's no oil here."

"Oh, yes," my father said, "you have lots of oil here, underground." He explained how, millions of years ago, this was a forest. They'd seen the petrified wood on Black Knoll? Some of the trees had turned to stone; others had sunk into the ground and turned into coal and oil. He loved to talk geology, even when the people listening couldn't understand a word.

Then a long silence fell, broken only by the pop of sticks in the fire.

One of the Navajos looked at us and said something.

My father asked Jimmy to translate. "He says he doesn't like you Anglos," Jimmy said.

The Navajos seemed to pull together in the firelight. Let's go, I kept thinking. Let's get out of here.

"He says you're always trying to take something from the Navajos."

"This isn't your land," my father said. "It belongs to Mr. Paulson. And you're burning one of his fenceposts."

I got ready to leap up—not to defend my father but to go for help. If I could outrun them.

"Once all this land belonged to the Navajos," Jimmy said. "Then you Anglos took it."

"That's right," my father said. "Kit Carson took it from you at the battle of Canyon de Chelly. You were great fighters. But you didn't have rifles. He took you prisoner and sent you to Fort Sumner. But your whole people walked back here together."

Jimmy spoke with one of the other Navajos; then he said, "You're right. He says his great-grandfather was on the Long Walk, and told him all about it."

The Navajos seemed impressed. They nodded several times and a more comfortable silence fell, while I wondered where my father had learned all this.

"It's hard for Navajos," Jimmy said. "Sometimes it seems like you Anglos got everything. All the Navajo has is his land. It's holy—every rock means something. Hank says you fought."

"Fought?" my father said. "Yes, I fought."

"I fought the Japs. I killed one of them with my bare hands. Maybe I shouldn't have done it. When I got back, I found my life was shortened. I started drinking. I really hated people and spent my time alone somewhere. You fought."

"Yes," my father said.

"So you know." Jimmy lit a cigarette from a glowing stick and took another drink.

"My father was what you call a medicine man. He told me the sickness I had was well known and would get me in a lot of trouble. I believe in some of the Navajo religion and some of the Anglo religion. He took me to a holy place. I breathed in and out four times, and every time I could feel the sickness leaving me. There was a storm coming. I painted a picture of this. That ceremony really blessed me. I sang all night long, and everything was beautiful."

He stood and tossed the empty bottle away. I heard it explode on the rocks, somewhere beyond the firelight.

"But now, I don't know. Things are not what I thought they'd be. I'm not a good farmer. All I want to do is paint. They"—he indicated the other Navajos—"think I'm stupid. I owe Hank a lot of money. But I don't make money painting, and sometimes I get sick again."

Another silence fell. Then one of the Navajos said something else.

"He wants to know if you're working for Washington," Jimmy said. "He thinks you're looking for this blasting powder the government uses to make the atomic bomb."

My father took the carnotite from the knapsack. "It looks like this," he said.

The Navajos passed it from hand to hand.

"Yes," Jimmy said, examining it carefully, "I've seen rock like this, long time ago—I don't remember the year. I was a boy, herding sheep near Sanhosteen. I went up a blind canyon and there was rock like this, lots of yellow rock."

He sounded like my father. It was strange to think your father looked at the world like an Indian.

Jimmy started to give it back. Their hands touched. "Keep it," my father said.

Before we left, the two of them stood for a moment, saying things I couldn't hear. Jimmy put his arms around my father and slapped his back. Boy, I thought, he's really loaded. The air outside the circle of firelight was cold. The other Navajos were still staring into the glowing fire, motionless as painted figures. Then we were walking again, toward the lights of the motel.

"Where'd you learn all that about Kit Carson?"

"At Fort Leavenworth Staff and Command School, when I was studying to get my captain's bars. I learned something in the army, Sonny; I didn't leave it a complete fool."

"What did he say to you?"

"Hell if I know. These Indians are the most sentimental people on the face of the earth. They should never let them drink. Do you know that boy is only thirteen years older than you? Terrible thing, what drinking does to them."

"I'm sorry about the Jeep."

"Don't worry about that," he said. "My work is done. I figured out where they should drill. Somewhere back along that road, the whole structure just sort of fell into place in my head."

We were getting close to the highway. Ahead, I could hear the soft roar of cars. "I was getting worried," I said. "For a while I thought we were going to have to spend the night out there."

"I slept in plenty of ditches in Europe," my father said.

A rig was brought in. By the second week, they reached the reservoir sandstone. The drill was stopped and samples brought up. Under ultraviolet light they were the yellow color of oil. But everyone already knew the well was going to be a big producer. The air around the rig was full of the odor of petroleum.

My father phoned Clint, who promised a big bonus. We drove to Gallup, and traded in our old car on a new Oldsmobile Rocket 88. It was turquoise and silver, like a piece of Navajo jewelry. Then we drove to Las Vegas, to meet Clint Yarborough for a big celebration. Before we left, my father went to the trading post and bought me the painting of the blue horse. The price had gone up to one hundred dollars.

In Las Vegas we stayed at the Desert Inn. It was like a big motel, with palm trees and a golf course. The bars were serving Atomic Cocktails. There was going to be a shot at the proving grounds the next morning. The papers said it was going to be one of the largest atomic bombs set off in the United States.

Clint Yarborough brought along a strange woman. He announced he was going to get a divorce and marry her. My mother took this hard. They took me to see Jack Benny and Gisele MacKenzie, then dropped me off and went out to party all night long. Sometime during the night, there was a terrible argument. My mother told me about it when they got back. I was already up and standing by the pool in my bathrobe, waiting for the bomb to go off.

"Your father told Clint Yarborough he didn't want to work for him," she said. She walked off toward their room. I saw my father coming slowly toward me, looking down at the ground.

The last seconds ticked off as we stood there together. In the flash, I saw on my father's face the same look of despair it always wore when he made money. To the north, what looked like the sun rose over the hills. People were shouting all over Las Vegas, but I stared at it calmly. I saw it as the release of billions of electron volts of energy, and felt no fear, only intense interest. My father had been right. Learn everything about what you feared, and you no longer feared it. In time, you could even learn to love it.

SIERRA WAVE

The first few months after Steve and Catherine were married, he felt full of a sort of glow, and was sometimes so happy he couldn't sleep. He would lay beside her all night, listening to her breathing, lost in the scent of her long, dark hair. In the early morning, before she woke, he would get up and tiptoe through the house, thinking of all the work he wanted to do to make it perfect, touching everything and saying little whispered prayers to himself, just like a kid, *Please, God, let it go on like this forever.*

There was only one disappointment. Catherine didn't like Joe, who lived in the house next door.

Joe was a stuntman who got along with all the Latinos on the block because he spoke perfect idiomatic Spanish. Steve liked him because he'd once been a jock himself. He thought Joe was one of the most interesting guys he'd ever met.

One day Joe took them out to the Burbank Studios to

watch him do a high fall. Shot by a narcotics squad cop, he fell backwards through a window and dropped seventy-five feet into an air bag. Later, while they were eating lunch in the studio commissary, Catherine told Joe she thought this was a childish way to make a living.

"You're right," he said. "It is childish." Then he looked at Steve and said, "When you were a kid, didn't you ever play at getting shot and killed?"

Steve told him yes, there had been a year when his childhood games of cowboys and Indians had concentrated on death scenes, the agonies of death.

"Same with me," Joe said. "Same with all boys. I read a book about this. Boys play with the idea of death—that's how they learn to deal with it. I'm still playing, that's all."

When they got back, Joe asked them to stop in for a beer. His home, like theirs, was high up on a hillside, and could be reached only by climbing an endless flight of steps. They sat on his porch and looked out over Echo Park.

The neighborhood had been built in the 1920s, then had been taken over by Latinos. Now, young Anglos like themselves were moving back in and buying the better homes. Steve liked Echo Park because here, everything he enjoyed about Los Angeles was heightened. The hills were steeper, the houses older, more mysterious. At night the streets still belonged to the gangs, and the police helicopter often circled overhead.

"Better put a stronger lock on your garage door," Joe told him. "Or your car won't last a month here."

"Have you been robbed?"

"No," Joe said. "Probably because they know I've got a gun."

Catherine said, "I've got a client who comes from around here. He's not such a bad kid." Catherine was a public defender for the Los Angeles County district attorney's office.

"What's he charged with?"

"Rape."

Joe nodded.

Steve knew Catherine was trying to make Joe angry. It was disappointing: His women had never gotten along with his male friends, but he'd thought Catherine would be different.

"What's his story?" Joe said.

"He says he met a woman in the parking lot of Ralph's who asked him to take her home and make love to her. Then she changed her mind and called the police."

"And you're going to get this guy off?"

"I'm going to try," Catherine said. "The problem is, he's too good-looking. The jury might decide he's telling the truth and convict him anyway."

Not long after that, she found an excuse to leave, as Steve had known she would.

"Your wife's a fine person, man," Joe said. "She's got high ideals and all. But if she believes that kid, she's dreaming." He stared out over the dry, brown hills. "I know these people. They'll smile to your face, then when you turn around, they'll put a knife in your back."

They talked for a while, about sports. Steve had been a big swimmer in college but he hadn't talked to anyone about it for a long time. He missed sports: Every so often, you had to hang it out and see what you could do.

"Let me show you something," Joe said. "I think you'll be interested."

Steve followed him into the garage. Suspended from the roof was a hang glider. He had never seen one this close before. It was smaller than he'd expected. He stared at the arching wings, aluminum tubes covered with bright red fabric.

"This is what I'm into now," Joe said. "You ever try it?"

Steve told him he'd thought about it.

"What stopped you?"

"I decided I'd rather do some real flying. You know, learn how to fly a real airplane."

"This is the real flying, brother."

Then Joe told him about hang gliding up north, in the Sierras—not just floating along a hundred feet above the beach, but standing on a mountaintop and catching the Sierra Wave, a thermal that could take you up to fourteen thousand feet, or higher, if you had the balls, so high you had to carry an oxygen bottle. He showed Steve a picture he'd taken of himself with a wingtip camera, dangling in his harness and grinning, the granite tops of mountains far below. The moment Steve saw that picture, he knew he had to learn.

Joe gave Steve lessons on the beach near Palos Verdes. Steve ran down a dune, holding the glider. As in certain dreams, his steps got longer and longer until he left the ground. At first the sensation frightened him; but he learned to enjoy it. Soon he was making slow turns, and Joe told him he showed promise. Then Joe took the glider, launched off a bluff, and floated far off down the coast and back.

When Steve got home, he started to tell Catherine, but she said, "I don't want to hear about it."

"Why not?"

"It's dangerous, isn't it? I don't see why you have to do everything Joe does. You look up to him like he was your older brother or something."

"That doesn't have anything to do with it," Steve said. It really wasn't that simple.

"You're going to get yourself killed. Or end up in a wheelchair for the rest of your life." She went into their bedroom and closed the door.

Steve went out in the garden and sat looking at the moon for a while. Of course it was dangerous. But in danger, you learned something about yourself.

He was sorry they couldn't get along. But there was no way they could have understood each other. Catherine believed in people. That was why she did what she did. She was always trying to help her clients, the ones she thought were worth helping. Joe believed only in himself.

That night, Steve had trouble sleeping again. Every time he closed his eyes, he felt his feet leaving the ground.

Steve had met Catherine at the end of a long period of drifting. He had started coming here, to Echo Park, getting back in touch with some people he had known slightly at Berkeley—ex-radicals who had ended up living here in the hills, dealing dope or writing screenplays.

One night someone had invited him to a party at Catherine's house. He had climbed the endless flight of stairs and found several people sitting on the porch, smoking hash and watching an eclipse of the moon.

At Berkeley, Catherine had been the lover of a radical named Josh who had been briefly as famous as a movie star. Since then, she had gone back to school, gotten a law degree, and moved here. Catherine wasn't like the others. She was keeping the promises, like she said—giving her clients books like *Soledad Brother*, so they could understand they were part of a historic struggle.

She told him she was happy here, except for one thing. Her house was for sale, and by the time she made enough money to afford it, it would belong to somebody else.

Steve hadn't met a girl like Catherine for years. He couldn't believe she lived alone, that she didn't have a lover. He fell in love with her at once. It took her a little longer to fall in love with him.

Two days after they'd met, it stormed. On an impulse he called her and said, "Let's go to the beach."

"Today?"

"Today's the best time."

So he took her to the beach and bodysurfed, showing off a little, and later they walked along the pier in the rain. "Thanks for bringing me," she said. "I haven't done anything like this for a long time."

But when he tried to hold her, she said, "No, I don't want that right now." When he asked her why, she told him, "I want us to stay friends."

So he held off. He took her out, but never made a move on her, or even talk to her that much. They went to the beach a lot. He would swim far out, then come back and find her lying on the sand, her face turned to the sun, her eyes closed. He felt she was beginning to enjoy herself. Still, nothing might have happened if they hadn't gone down to San Diego that weekend.

She had asked him to drive her down and pick up some things from her mother's. It was the sort of favor you asked of a friend, but he had done it. On the way back, he had decided to stop in and see his parents. Catherine had gotten very quiet when she had seen the house.

Steve's father was a retired admiral, now on the

board of a big aerospace corporation. His mother's family owned half the timber in Northern California. They'd had drinks on the patio. His parents had done most of the talking, as usual, but Catherine had held her own. His mother had been so impressed she even asked them to stay for dinner. Then his parents had gone into the house and left Steve and Catherine alone.

"You should have told me about this," she said.

"What's that?"

"You know what I'm talking about. All this money."

"I'm not like my parents," he said. "We don't even get along. I haven't been home in a year."

"I'm sorry I found out," she said. "I hate people who have money."

Suddenly he realized she was drunk.

"It doesn't mean that much," he said.

"Not to you. You've got it." She leaned forward. "You don't work, do you? I wondered why you never had anything to do except go to the beach. You've never had to do a thing you didn't want to do. I guess you thought I'd jump into bed with you when I saw this house. Well, it's not going to work."

She dropped her drink. It fell to the patio and broke. "Shit," she said, stooping over to pick up the pieces.

"Don't bother."

"You know something?" she said. "I feel sorry for you. You're almost thirty. What in the hell have you been doing with yourself all these years?"

"Maybe," he said, "I was waiting for you."

"Oh hell," she said. "Just get me out of here. Just take me home."

Halfway back to Los Angeles, it began to rain. Catherine sat next to him, saying nothing. He wanted to throw her out of the car. On the radio he began hearing bulletins about the storm that was moving in over the Los Angeles basin. It was the worst storm in years. There were reports of flooding, landslides; everyone was advised to stay at home. From the time they passed Anaheim they were locked in hopeless traffic. When they were almost downtown, Steve saw red flares burning on the road ahead, a big semi jackknifed across the road.

The highway patrolman who was directing traffic told him the Hollywood exit, which would take them to Echo Park, was closed. Steve, desperate to get rid of Catherine, took it anyway. When he got to the intersection of Fargo and Alvarado, he saw water pouring across the road ahead. He hit the brakes, but he was going too fast. The Audi ploughed into the water and the motor died.

Catherine gave a yell as the floor of the car filled with cold water, and tried to open her door. Steve grabbed her, locking his fists in the pit of her stomach. She was shouting at him, trying to scratch his face. Then the tires broke loose, and for a few moments of absolute terror they were floating, until the Audi came to rest, sideways against a telephone pole.

The headlights went out. Heavy drops of rain pounded the roof. They sat there, listening to water pour around the tires and into the mouth of the storm drain. "I'm sorry," Catherine said.

"I should have let you drown," he said. He told her more, everything he'd been holding back for weeks.

Then he was finished. His shoes were full of water and his face hurt.

"Can't we get to a telephone?" Catherine said.

"We're not going anyplace."

"Then there's nothing to do?"

"Nothing to do but wait."

Catherine smiled. She took off her shoes. Then she rolled down her pantyhose and balled them up and put them in the glove compartment. She smiled again. "Have you ever," she asked Steve, "made love in a car?"

Three weeks later they were married, and the week after that Steve bought her house in Echo Park.

Joe decided it was time for Steve to solo. Catherine wanted to come along, too, so early one Sunday morning they loaded the hang glider into Joe's pickup and drove to the beach.

Along the top of the bluff there was what Joe called a rotor, a rolling cylinder of air. By staying in the rotor you could fly a couple of miles down the beach. Joe told him not to go out of sight, not on his first flight.

"Aren't you going to use the parachute?" Catherine said.

Joe, who never wore his parachute, said, "It doesn't matter. He won't be high enough for it to open."

Steve walked to the edge of the cliff. He tossed off orange peels, and watched the rotor carry them back up and into the blinding eye of the sun.

"Don't do this," Catherine said. "You're scared, I can tell."

"That's not a good thing to say right now," Joe said.

As he buckled on the parachute, Steve was sorry Catherine had come.

Joe handed him the crash helmet. "Remember," he said. "The ground is your enemy."

"I know."

"Do good."

Steve lifted the glider and hooked in. Standing on the edge of the dropoff, he wondered for a moment why he

was doing this; then Joe's instructions took over and he
ran forward until his feet left the ground.

His groin was tingling and his throat felt like it was
full of hot pins. Dimly he could hear Joe yelling for him to
get the nose down. Then Joe's voice faded out, and the
only sound was the variometer tone, rising and falling as
he gained or lost altitude. He shifted his body to the left
and made a slow turn to the south.

Now he was flying along the bluff. He knew he
should turn back soon, but he was beginning to lose his
fear. Steve had not been prepared for how much he could
see. He watched his shadow slip along over rooftops,
parking lots, telephone lines. The ground began to take
on such detail it seemed that even if he fell, he could not
be hurt. Only one person noticed him. A woman sunbath-
ing beside a mobile home, who lifted her beer can as he
passed over. Steve felt sorry for the people on the ground.
At three hundred feet, he could see beyond the horizons
that kept them all in their ordered paths, like the cars
following the simple grid of streets.

On the way back, a seagull flew alongside him for a
time. Then he saw Joe's pickup, and his heart began to
pound again. Landing was the most delicate part.

He came down, into the layer of warm air close to
the ground that was full of the smell of dirt and traffic
noises, hitting so hard he fell to his knees.

Joe was pounding his shoulder. "How long was I
up?" he asked him.

"Six minutes."

It had seemed much longer.

When Steve got out of his harness, Catherine put her
arms around him and held him for a long time. "I was so
frightened," she said. "You weren't supposed to go out of
sight."

Catching sight of his reflection in the mirror of Joe's pickup, Steve thought he looked better than he had ever looked in his life. He told Joe that pretty soon he'd be ready to catch one of those big thermals.

"Take it easy, brother," Joe laughed. "You got a long way to go before you can take that old Swallowtail up in a thermal. But you were looking good," he added seriously. "You were looking real good."

Instead of taking them home, Joe insisted they go to a bar he knew of in El Monte for a celebration. It was called La Azteca, and when they came in the *vatos* at the pool table gave them dirty looks. But Joe got along with everyone because he spoke that perfect idiomatic Spanish. They sat in a booth, eating a plate of shrimps and drinking tequila, and Joe told them stories of growing up around here, when his father had worked for Lockheed and he had run with the gangs. "They treat you right here," Catherine said.

"They all know me," Joe said. "I come back here two or three times a year. They're my people."

Steve was enjoying everthing. His sunburned face, Joe's approval, this bar. He felt he had won a contest with himself. They would come here often.

"The only thing I can't understand," Catherine said, "is why you're so conservative, growing up the way you did."

"Hey," Joe said. "Your husband's had a good day. He doesn't want to talk about politics. Why don't you let it go?"

"Right, honey," Steve said. "Let it go."

After that, Catherine stopped putting Joe down. She seemed to have decided she could tolerate him. Joe, on the other hand, started to really like her. He told Steve he was fortunate to have such a smart, good-looking wife.

One morning he and Joe started for the beach in Joe's pickup, telling Catherine they'd be gone all day. But halfway there, the pickup began to overheat. The thermostat was broken. Joe found a parts store and bought another one, but by that time it was getting late, so they decided to go back to Echo Park.

Joe dropped Steve off, saying he'd be over in a minute for a beer, and Steve climbed the steps. Something about the silence bothered him when he came through the back door. It was as if the whole house was holding its breath.

He stopped in the kitchen, looking through the door into the dining room. Reflected in the mirror over the table, he could see the front room, and on the couch, something that did not belong. Suddenly it resolved itself into two people. A man and a woman. His wife lying under another man.

His heart was pounding, but still he did not move. He stared, the sight of them pouring into him, knowing he would never forget this. He knew what he was seeing, but at the same time he struggled to understand it, to sort it out. The man was lying between her legs, his lips to her ear. And through all this, there was silence, until Catherine made a little sound in the back of her throat.

He must have shifted his weight. The floor cracked, and suddenly the figures jumped into life. But he was already moving, coming around the corner, saying something, he didn't know what. Then the man was on his feet and holding a knife.

For an endless moment, nobody moved. He could see the man very clearly in the sunlight falling through the living room windows. He was a Latino, young, a boy really, with a dark, narrow face and tangled black hair. Catherine had drawn up her knees and hidden her eyes with her hand. She made another little sound Steve thought was a sob.

The boy came toward him. Steve couldn't take his eyes off the knife. He had the feeling he'd seen it before, perhaps in a pawnshop window. It had a red plastic handle and a long, shining blade. The boy picked up the telephone and cut the cord. It took him a couple of tries.

He could have gone for the knife while the boy was hopping around, pulling on his pants. But that would have brought things to a conclusion, and he didn't want to know what was happening to him yet. Ahead was pain beyond anything he had imagined. So he stayed in the present, his ears ringing and his mouth dry.

Just before he went to the door, the boy put a finger to his lips. It was supposed to mean. Don't say a word about this. Steve knew, because they were so close he could read his thoughts. He also knew that in some terrible way, they would now be close forever.

He got as far as the porch. Then Joe was coming up the steps, taking two and three steps at a time. The boy dropped the knife but Joe picked up a pair of garden shears and hit him across the forehead anyway; hit him again, yelling, until he went down.

The cops came, handcuffed the boy, and took him down to their car. Steve sat on the back porch, Joe's arm around his shoulders, and cried like a baby. After a while one of the cops came out and told him he could see Catherine.

She was sitting on the bed, wearing her robe. "You should go to the hospital," he said.

"I'm all right," she said. "He hadn't started yet. He

was telling me what he was going to do." She closed her eyes.

Steve felt as if the room was flying away from him.

"I still think you should go to the hospital," he said. "If you're going to press charges."

"There's a problem," she said. "I know him. That was Miguel, the boy I was defending. On the rape charge," she added, laughing.

He sat down on the bed beside her. "Tell me what happened," he said.

"He's a very confused boy," she said. "He showed up and said he wanted to talk about his testimony. He's come here before. I didn't tell you because I didn't want to upset you. Then he told me he loved me. He told me he'd been in love with me for a long time." She cleared her throat. "I tried to talk to him. I didn't realize how dangerous the situation was."

He stared at the floor. "If it were another woman, you'd tell her to press charges."

"You don't understand. His lawyer would just make it look like I encouraged him."

"There was the knife."

"There was the knife, but I compromised myself when I let him come here. His lawyer could make me look like a fool."

Steve didn't know what to say. It seemed wrong to him, all wrong.

"Look," she said, "I'm not hurt. If I press charges, only two things can happen—one, my reputation gets destroyed, and two, he goes to jail for five or ten years. And I don't want him to have to go through that. I don't hate him. I just don't ever want to see him again."

She stood up. "The best thing to do is just put it behind us. But thank God for Joe."

"Yes," he said. "Thank God for Joe."

*　　*　　*

The next morning, Catherine decided she should go to work. So she drove off to the Hall of Justice and Steve was left alone.

He walked through the empty house, remembering he'd considered knocking out a wall to enlarge the bedroom. Finding a hammer, he stood before the wall for a long time. Then he hit it as hard as he could, and the head of the hammer sank through the plaster. The blow released some kind of energy. When Catherine came home, he was still working.

The morning after that he decided there was no reason to stop with the bedroom. It was time to do all the things he had wanted to do with the house. Before he could stop himself, he went out and bought hundreds of feet of lumber. Then he began knocking out the back wall.

As he worked, he thought about what had happened. He couldn't stop seeing them lying on the couch. The night after it had happened, he had dreamed he had come in and seen two snakes coiling together.

Now he brought the image back to life. It was still there, so clear the figures seemed cut out of metal. But certain details bothered him. The knife, for instance. Had it been there all along, or had Miguel only taken it out of his pocket when he jumped up? No, he thought, there had been no knife, not when he had first seen them.

There had been her throat, but no knife, her head thrown back in a complete lack of resistance that was totally unlike her. Her eyes closed, her legs thrown apart. She looked as he had seen her when she lay on the sand, eyes closed, giving herself up to the sun, enjoying her own pleasure. Remembering this, he felt his blood stir with some massive inevitability; the same feeling he had when he saw a big wave coming toward him.

175

*   *   *

He had to talk to someone, so he called up Joe and asked him if he'd like to go to the beach. It was too cold to swim so they sat in Joe's pickup, drinking, until it got dark.

"I hate to see this guy get off too," Joe said. "But maybe she's right. Why put her through it?"

"She should have pressed charges," Steve said.

Joe put his hand on his shoulder. "Know what's wrong with you, brother?"

"What?"

"You didn't do anything to help her. You want to get over this? Take this guy out for good."

"Take him out?" Steve said.

Joe leaned close. "There's ways," he said urgently. "You don't want to do it yourself, there's people who can do it for you. I know these people. I'll put you in touch with them."

"You could do that?"

"Sure," Joe said. "She's worth it."

Steve thought about this.

"You got a woman worth doing anything for," Joe said, "then you do what needs to be done."

"No," Steve said, after a while. "I don't think I could go for that."

"It's your call," Joe said, starting the pickup. "But you'd better think about this. That guy's out on the streets. He could come back around any time."

The next week, Catherine told Steve she was going to start carrying a gun.

"But that's just what you used to put Joe down for," he said.

"Joe was right about a lot of things."

*   *   *

Joe belonged to a gun club. On Sunday morning they drove out to the foothills above Chatsworth. The club was set back from the road, behind a fence topped with coils of barbed wire. Joe had his own key.

They walked up a long, dry arroyo to the combat firing range. From a toolbox, Joe took out his nickel-plated Colt .45 and showed Catherine how to hold it in a tight isometric grip for greater accuracy.

Like all martial arts, Joe said, shooting was a matter of concentration. You knew what you were doing. The other guy didn't. The idea was to stay in control, one step ahead of the other guy. He pressed a foot switch and paper silhouettes of people traveled across in front of them on a line. Catherine shot as well as she did everything else. She stood with feet slightly apart, carefully squeezing off each round.

"Put 'em in the A Box," Joe said. "Head, heart, and lungs."

The pistol made a flat, liquid pop that stung Steve's ears. After every clip, Joe inspected the silhouettes. It was just like karate, he said. Knowing you could kill someone made it possible not to, except as a last resort. Still, looking at the holes torn in the silhouettes, it was difficult not to imagine what the bullets could do to a real human being.

They came home and built a fire and had some supper. "So," Catherine said. "Can you get me a gun?"

"I can get you a good little gun," Joe said. "One you can carry in your purse. But there's more to it than hitting the target. You've got to develop confidence and concentration. The most important thing is determining the threat. What I'm saying is, it's all in knowing when to use it."

"Then I don't see the good of it," Steve said.

They looked at him.

"If you think about it, having a gun wouldn't have helped you. Let's look at what happened," he said. "He came to the door and you let him in. You didn't think there was anything wrong."

"Please," Catherine said. "Don't make me go through it again. I don't want to think about it."

She got up and left the room.

Joe shook his head.

"I'll walk you home," Steve said.

It was cold, and a light rain had begun to fall. They stopped under the streetlight at the top of the hill.

"Look," Joe said. "She asked me to teach her how to shoot. I'm just trying to help. And while we're at it, why the hell do you keep bringing up what happened?"

Steve stared at the streetlight.

"She told me you're always asking her about it," Joe said. "That ain't helping, man. What's the point of it?"

Steve said nothing, but Joe must have been able to read his thoughts.

"You don't think this guy is innocent, do you?" Joe said.

Steve felt a wave of shame go through him, so intense that his body tingled and again he felt hot pins in his throat, as if he had just launched himself into space.

"You sonofabitch," Joe said softly. "I can't believe it. You're the one who should be on her side. You of all people. You've lost it, buddy."

He walked away and left Steve standing there, alone under the streetlight.

Joe never mentioned the conversation again, but after that there was a certain coldness between them. Then Joe went off to Arizona on location.

It rained every day. The work on the house went

slowly. Catherine had trouble sleeping. Whole days went by when they hardly spoke.

Catherine had begun to seem like a stranger to Steve. Sometimes he felt he knew nothing about her, never had. He knew it was wrong to doubt Catherine, and on one level he did not; but on another level, his doubts were out of control. It was strange, like being two people at once. And when he was that other person, he couldn't stop himself from asking her to go through it again, to tell him exactly how it had happened. Then the morning came when she said to him, "You don't believe me, do you?"

"I want to," he said. "But why didn't you press charges?" She looked at him with that calm gray look that meant she had been taking her sleeping pills.

"You want me to tell you I was fucking him, don't you? You poor bastard," she said, turning away. "I feel sorry for you."

So his doubts were known. He supposed they showed. He would never know what really happened, but he was sure of one thing. He had lost her. She no longer loved him.

It was raining, but Steve went out on the roof. Taking a nail from his apron pocket, he drove it with careful blows of the hammer, concentrating on a picture of his house the way he wanted it to be.

But finally the rain stopped, and one night he came home and found Catherine crying. She let him hold her for a long time. The next day she seemed to feel better, and Steve began to think they would somehow forget what she had said. Then one morning not long after that Joe showed up at the front door, back from location, with a bottle of tequila and a big smile on his face. Steve asked him what this was all about.

"You forgotten, man?" Joe said. "It's your birthday."

Joe gave him a dexedrine tablet so he could finish the house, and Catherine gave him a big pair of taps, which he nailed on his shoes and then danced around the kitchen, like Bill Bojangles Robinson. Then Joe said he'd get his girl, and they could all go to La Azteca.

Joe's girl lived in North Hollywood, an actress, not too bright, that he'd met on location. They sat around her pool, had some drinks, and smoked a joint. When it got dark, they started for El Monte. Steve could tell Catherine was disappointed in Joe's girl, but what had she expected?

When they walked into the bar, all the *vatos* stared at Joe's girl, who was wearing a little red top that showed everything. For a while they sat in a booth, Catherine arguing with Joe, who was a Catholic, about abortion, then Steve asked Joe's girl if she'd like to play pool.

He'd forgotten the taps. They clicked when he walked to the pool table. Joe's girl was talking about the Industry, meaning the movie industry, and Steve pretended he thought she meant the auto industry. "What do you do?" she asked him. He told her, "I'm a professional carpenter."

Then the *vatos* came over, kidding him about his shoes, and Steve got a little nervous. But it turned out all right. He spoke Spanish—it helped being stoned—and told them it was his birthday. They started shooting pool with Joe's girl so they could watch her lean over the table. She seemed to be enjoying herself, so Steve went to the bar.

"*Cerveza por todos mis amigos*," he told the bartender.

"You having a good time?"

"A very good time," Steve said. "This is a great place you've got here."

"You a friend of Joe's?"

"*Si*," Steve said. "Joe is my *amigo*."

"Joe and his wife, they come here all the time," the bartender said, nodding toward the booth where Joe and Catherine were sitting.

"No, that's my wife," Steve said. "The woman sitting with Joe is my wife."

The bartender glanced at his helper, who had been listening. Steve thought he smiled slightly.

"And a tequila for myself," Steve said.

The bartender put the drink on the bar with fast little moves, not too polite. The more Steve thought about it, he was certain the bartender had smiled.

Steve looked at Joe and Catherine sitting in the booth. Their eyes were locked together. Joe's fingers slid down the side of his glass. Catherine stroked the long, dark hair that hung down the side of her face, over and over. Her head was thrown back and her lips formed careful expressions. They seemed to both be moving together, ever so slowly.

It came to him that for some time now, Catherine had stopped speaking about Joe altogether.

You're stoned, he thought. You're seeing things. It's not true.

But he knew that it was true. Even if it hadn't happened yet, it would. The way their bodies moved together didn't lie.

In June, Joe started talking about taking a trip up north, to the Owens Valley, so Steve could do some real soaring. Catherine wasn't against the idea. In fact, he had the feeling they'd talked about it.

They drove north in Joe's pickup, through the Mojave, until the Sierras rose up on their left. Catherine sat between them, talking about how good it was to get out of the city. They spent that night in a campground outside of Bishop.

Joe built a fire, and as they watched the sun go down, he remarked that the air up here was so clear you could see for a hundred miles.

Then Steve said, "Yeah, you can see a lot from up here," and in the silence that followed, he felt they all knew each other's thoughts.

More than anything else, he wanted to talk about it. But Catherine said she was tired and went into their tent. Joe just stared at the fire. Steve waited for him to say something, but when, after long minutes had gone by, he still hadn't, Steve began to feel something he had never thought he would feel for Joe. Contempt.

"You know something?" he said finally. "You're not who I thought you were."

Then he got his sleeping bag and walked off into the darkness. The wind woke him just before daybreak. He stood and looked at the mountains, feeling today would be the day they had all been waiting for.

They drank coffee, folded the tent, and put it in the back of the pickup. As they drove up the dirt road to the top of Gunter Peak, Joe said it was going to be a hot day, a good day for soaring.

The mountaintop was a dry world of exposed rock and brilliant sunlight. Here and there were trees that looked dead, distorted, as if they had been struck by lightning. Joe explained they were bristlecone pines, and they could be a thousand years old.

Steve walked around, stopping to watch a kid with long yellow hair assemble his glider. "How you doing?" the kid asked him.

"Fine," Steve said. "It's going to be a great day. Going to catch one of those big thermals today."

The kid put down his tools and gave Steve a long look. "You done much of this?" he said.

182

"No," Steve admitted. "Not a lot."

"Then you'd better be careful of those thermals. They're nothing to fool around with."

Steve said he'd be careful and walked on, thinking how different the kid talked from Joe, who always made it sound like it was one big game.

Joe and Catherine were standing by one of the pines. They flipped a coin to see who would go first. Steve won, and Joe went to finish assembling the glider.

"Everything's going to be different from now on," Steve said to Catherine.

She looked at him strangely.

"What do you mean?"

"You know what I mean," he said, taking her hand. "Everything is going to be clean and out in the open."

He could feel her looking at him as he walked to the glider.

Joe was working slowly, as if he had second thoughts. "Maybe you'd better take it easy today," he said.

"Take it easy?"

"Maybe you'd better not try for a thermal yet. Just take a short hop. It's up to you."

"All right," Steve said.

"Then you won't be needing the oxygen bottle. Do you want the parachute?"

"No, I won't be needing the parachute either."

Joe gave him an approving nod. They carried the glider to the dropoff, and Steve hooked in. "Wait until you feel warm air coming up the slope," Joe said, "then go for it."

Steve looked back at Catherine, standing by the dead tree. She lifted her hand. Then he felt warm air on his face. He ran forward until it caught the airfoil, and lifted off into space.

The sunlight was blinding. The mountaintop fell away. A mile ahead, he could see several gliders turning together, and headed for them. It was a thermal. He knew it the moment he felt the strong upward push. Forgetting all caution, he gave himself to it completely. One by one the other gliders dropped out. Then there was only a bird, perhaps an eagle, and together they spiraled for thousands of feet, straight up into the sun.

When the cold began to bite, even through his down jacket, Steve pulled the control bar back into his stomach. But the glider did not respond. The thermal was irresistible. He tried everything, even put both feet onto the bar, but the glider continued climbing. Then he did what he had been afraid to do until now. He looked down.

Thousands of square miles were spread out at his feet, like a topographic map. He was higher than the highest mountains now. They looked like piles of gray cement. The little lakes between them were frozen. The detail was astonishing. Looking south, he saw Mount Whitney. He could follow the highway back down the valley, through Bishop and Lone Pine and Big Pine. He could see all the way to China Lake. But something was wrong. He saw everything as if through the wrong end of a telescope. Detailed, distant, surrounded by a halo of blackness. He had flown so high he was suffering from lack of oxygen. He was losing consciousness. But he could see so far, and so much, that he felt a joy stronger than any he had ever known. Dangling in the sun, he felt tears streaming down his face, and knew only that he was floating, he was flying.

HB 10 T